Do Not
Go Gentle

C.A. Larmer is a journalist, editor, teacher and author of multiple crime series, stand-alone novels and a non-fiction book about pioneering surveyors in Papua New Guinea. Christina grew up in PNG, was educated in Australia, and spent many years working in Sydney, London, Los Angeles and New York. She now lives with her musician husband, boomerang sons and their very cheeky Bluey on the east coast of Australia.

Sign up for news, views and giveaways:
calarmer.com

ALSO BY C.A. LARMER

The Posthumous Mystery series:
Do Not Go Alone

The Murder Mystery Book Club series:
The Murder Mystery Book Club (Book 1)
Danger On the SS Orient (Book 2)
Death Under the Stars (Book 3)
When There Were 9 (Book 4)
The Widow on the Honeymoon Cruise (Book 5)
Gone Guest (Book 6)

The Ghostwriter Mystery series:
Killer Twist (Book 1)
A Plot to Die For (Book 2)
Last Writes (Book 3)
Dying Words (Book 4)
Words Can Kill (Book 5)
A Note Before Dying (Book 6)
Without a Word (Book 7)

The Sleuths of Last Resort:
Blind Men Don't Dial Zero
Smart Girls Don't Trust Strangers
Good Girls Don't Drink Vodka

PLUS
*After the Ferry: A Gripping
Psychological Novel*

An Island Lost

C.A. LARMER

Do Not
Go Gentle

LARMER MEDIA

Published by Larmer Media
NSW Australia
www.calarmer.com
ISBN: 978-0-9942608-6-4
Cover design by Stuart Eadie

for my beautiful boys,
Nimo and Felix

PROLOGUE

So there's been a murder. My murder, in fact, but please don't waste time feeling sorry for me. Your tears and platitudes are of no use to me now. I need your help to solve this thing, and I need it fast. I'll explain why shortly, but for now, let's try to iron out the facts while they're still clear in my mind.

I'm dead. Stabbed just once from behind, but gee it did the job. Hence the reason I need your help. I never saw the bugger coming. I have no idea who did this to me or why. I have no idea what he used, but I recall something cold and sharp before it all went black. A knife most likely, but let's not jump to conclusions too quickly.

I'm currently lying in a sticky pool of my own blood. Well, I can only assume it's sticky. Certain senses are no longer available to me, and that's a good thing. Believe you me, nobody wants to *feel* their own blood oozing out of their body, coagulating beneath them, turning dark and pungent. Again, that's just an assumption. I've seen enough *CSI* to know how it works. Thank God I didn't lose control of my bowels. That would have been embarrassing. For now, I've left a pretty clean corpse.

Not a bad-looking one either, if I do say so myself.

I'm only thirty-eight, after all. I have a thick mop of hair, the colour of maple syrup. I have faintly tanned legs, which are sprawled rather delicately on the floor, just a sliver of black undies showing beneath my red-and-white spotted nightdress, a larger red splotch where the murder weapon entered my back. Really, it just looks like five dots have joined together for a group hug. Nothing too alarming, I can assure you of that.

So I've been stabbed. By person or persons unknown. The cops have no idea yet. No one does, which is where you come in.

If death has taught me one thing, it's that we have to be quick. I see a light. I see a tunnel. I see my dead grandmother beckoning like there's no tomorrow—which I guess, for me, there isn't—but I won't have it. I need to know who did this to me, and I'm guessing the well-lit, granny-beckoning tunnel won't wait long.

I'm guessing we've got two hours, maybe three. Tops.

So I'm going to fill you in on the facts leading up to my death and the drama that unfolds. I'm going to give you as much detail as I can without sending you on a wild-goose chase or leaving you wanting to stick another knife in my back. I have my suspicions, I have my theories, but I'll try not to prejudice you with those. I need you to think about this clearly and objectively, and I need you to tell me as quickly as possible *whodunit*. Not because I can do anything about it. I'm not delusional—death is death is death, after all—but because I need to know, before I choof off into eternity, that my thirteen-year-old son did not murder me.

Damn it, I wasn't going to do that.

Sorry.

But here's the thing: I have a sneaky, dreadful, gut-wrenching suspicion my only child is the culprit. He's my prime suspect, and it breaks my heart. Or it would if my heart wasn't already broken, pierced with that cold, sharp weapon that I can only assume is a knife but which you mustn't jump to conclusions about. Gee I'm really stuffing this up, aren't I?

So here's how it's going to work. I'm going to help you out as best I can. I don't know all the rules yet—this death thing is new, you got that, right? But I'm learning pretty quickly that I have a fairly decent bird's-eye view of the crime scene. As far as I can tell at this early stage, I can see most things. I'm nowhere yet everywhere all at once. Omnipresent I think they call it. I appear to be floating above, but I can move around too. Kind of like my son's drone, I hover above, beside, into and through. Having said that, I can't quite access everything. For some strange reason, I can only see into certain parts of my house; I'm not sure what that's about. There must be method in Death's madness, but it's a little maddening to be honest. Still, I'm in a pretty good position to work this out, and you, dear reader, are my conduit.

Do you mind?

It's not like I'm asking you to get your hands dirty or put yourself in harm's way. Hell, you can't even get in there and poke and prod, but what you can do, what I need most right now, is for you to be my sounding board. Be there to help me sort fact from fiction. I don't want to do this alone. I need someone to bear witness, someone to know I tried. And I want that someone to be very much alive.

So I ask for just a few hours of your time. Help me sift through the suspects, climb all over the clues. Help me deduce, beyond a reasonable doubt, that it wasn't my son—my achingly beautiful son—who murdered me in cold blood, and I will be eternally grateful. And I mean that quite literally, of course.

Help me work out whodunit before that bloody light extinguishes all hope of ever knowing.

And good luck!

CHAPTER 1

My son was born prematurely, a difficult birth, an agonising start. I know we haven't much time, but bear with me, this will come in handy later. I just know it will. He was tiny, but I was tiny too. Always had been, apart from a slight blip during my boozy university years when all that cheap cider left its mark. So by week thirty of my pregnancy, my hips had carked it and I was wobbling about like a beer-bellied old lady with a walking stick.

When you're able-bodied, you tend to begrudge all those empty wheelie car parks right out the front of every supermarket, shopping centre, and cinema complex, and you might even have considered sneaking into one. But once you actually *need* a wheelie car park, well good luck finding one, my friend! Suddenly they're all taken and you have to hobble three kilometres just to buy a loaf of bread.

And don't even start me on ramp access.

So I hobbled about until week thirty-eight when the obstetrician decided my penance was complete and booked me in to be induced.

"It'll be over before you know it!" he'd promised in that smug *I've never had a child, but I'm somehow more of an expert than you* way. But he was wrong.

After twenty-six and a half hours of excruciating labour, they finally agreed to give me an epidural, and my tiny child was suctioned out of me an hour after that.

It took another twelve hours before I could feel my

legs again and, I guess, even longer for bub to discover his lips because he didn't latch on at all to start with. He didn't seem to have a clue. I could only deduce he was as bombed out of his brain as I was.

As a consequence, for the first few months, feeding was a disaster. It's like we both missed the How To class and couldn't catch up.

Every two hours for weeks on end it was our mini battleground. I would shove him on, he'd spit me out, and my husband would chuckle beside us. He seemed to find it all so amusing, not sensing how crippling it felt. How mortifying. How *unwomanly*.

"Just give him the bottle," he said over and over, meaning, *He clearly doesn't want you.*

He might as well have stabbed me in my left breast.

Then one day I awoke to my son's usual hungry squawks and I thrust him to my breast as I always did, tensing for the inevitable trauma, but it never came.

He simply latched on and began to gently suckle. It was like every bird was singing in unison, every flower blossoming at once. It was one giant, tacky cliché, and I loved it. In that one simple act of acceptance, my entire life shifted. By latching onto me, my son and I became one again.

And that's when my husband latched onto someone else.

At first I never suspected a thing. He disappeared at all hours, for many hours at a time. Came back and headed straight for the shower, that kind of thing. So obvious, so cliché, and yet I honestly didn't twig. I certainly didn't put two and two together and come up with a couple that didn't include *moi*. I guess I was too busy with Bob.

Did I tell you I called my son Bob?

It's a very ordinary name, sure, but that was the whole point. There were enough loony names in my family already. I wasn't going to saddle my child with another.

Bob's dad's name is Cassowary. Yep, that's his first

name. Do you see what I'm saying? Loony. I should have run a mile the first time he said it to me, over a greasy bacon omelette after a torrid one-night stand. Or at least it was supposed to be. We'd not even bothered to exchange names that night, just stumbled to my apartment together after hitting it off in that Irish dive not far from my place. Neither of us expected it to go anywhere, of course. But when he was still there the next morning and our stomachs were growling in unison, he suggested we hit a café, and I didn't bother to decline.

What the hell, I was hungry.

"I'm Cassowary," he'd said, midmouthful, and I had laughed.

When he didn't laugh along, I choked back my chortle and said, "What? Really? Like the animal?"

"It's a flightless bird, actually. Native to Papua New Guinea." His frown had remained in place, like no one had ever had a bad reaction to his really stupid name before.

"Oh, right. And your surname?" I was going to add, "Is it Emu?" But something about his frozen frown stopped me.

"Jones."

"Of course."

Cassowary Jones. I kid you not. That was—is—his name, and I stayed around to finish my eggs. I can see you're losing respect for me already. Never mind, that's not essential to solve this thing.

So where was I? That's right: We ate spongy omelettes, and I told him my name was Ludovica Gold but that everyone calls me Lulu. Then I did what I always do and paused so he could have a good ole laugh. Yep. I've got a loony name too, but at least I *know* it's loony. At least I don't act all surprised when people hesitate, then widen their eyes and say, "Huh?"

I've learned to smile patiently, to shrug my shoulders, to add, "What can I say? My mother's a bit batty."

The truth is, my mother is relatively sane, but she had a

blind spot for a mad Bavarian King called Ludwig someone-or-other, who happened to build a Cinderella-style castle back in the late 1800s. Seems after traipsing through it on her honeymoon, Mum couldn't get the joint out of her system, and I was now stuck with it for life, named after the mad King Ludwig (or the feminine form at least). Of course I didn't tell him all that, at least not then. Nobody needs to hear the snoring details of my stupid name.

In any case, we were two ridiculously named one-night standers who really should have parted company that first night and, failing that, never called each other again after breakfast. But for some bizarre reason, one I will never understand—even now with the wisdom of hindsight—we agreed to meet again, that night, back at my place. We didn't bother with the dingy pub this time. We knew what we wanted, and we wanted it over and over until, a few months down the track, the inevitable happened and I fell pregnant.

Cut to nine months later via a rushed marriage, and Bob Gold was born. I know what you're thinking. Why doesn't he have his father's surname? Well, I have to ask, why should he? I didn't take the name Jones. Plus when you think about it, it's really the woman who does all the hard yakka. Sure, he squirts something in, but I'm the one who had to bake and ache for nine months, and don't forget the trauma of childbirth (twenty-six-and-a-half hours of excruciating pain in case you had). I'm the one who cooked him up, the one left holding the stinky nappies while my so-called "partner" did a runner. It's just as well I gave Bob my surname.

Sure, maybe if I'd allowed Cass (no way was I referring to him as a flightless bird; the bugger took flight at the first opportunity) some kind of ownership of his son, maybe he might not have looked elsewhere for validation. I guess I'll never know. Not sure I really care, but that's beside the point.

In any case, one night I awoke and found Cass had vanished from our bed. Bob was snuffling away on the duvet beside me, and I glanced around, more curious than concerned. Was Cass in the spare bed again, a place he frequently slinked off to, more interested in sleep than bonding with his son? Or was he downstairs pretending to scrutinise the share market while scrounging for porn on the web?

Either would have been preferable to what I had soon discovered. Through the window, within easy sight of our bedroom, was my husband in another bedroom, in another bed. He was directly across the road at a stranger's house. Or at least she was a stranger to *me*. I had to assume he knew her, judging by their proximity to each other, their nudity, and the giant smile on her face. The lights were on. The neighbour had him in a chokehold that almost saw me dialling 000 before I realised he was smiling too. They were *in flagrante*, and he was enjoying every minute. Worse, he kept darting glances towards my window. Yep, seriously. No way he could have seen me, no way he could know I was awake and watching, wide-eyed and mortified in the dark. But on they went, her smiling, him staring smugly towards me. Sick bastard.

So what did I do?

I turned over and went back to sleep, of course. I had a baby to feed in four hours, and I was damned if I was going to let him ruin Bob's breakfast. Then when he left for work the next day, all cutesy kisses and chirpy whistle, I placed all his belongings in the back incinerator and burned them to a crisp, hired a locksmith to change the locks, and left a note on the front door telling him to bugger off.

And bugger off he did, straight to the floozy across the road where they continued to make love with the curtains open and the lights bright for the first year or so, her smiling less each time, and him still glancing towards our window, his expression increasingly inscrutable.

Eventually they closed the blinds.

So why am I sharing this sordid little chapter in my sorry little life? Well, I guess either of them could be the culprit. I guess you could pin it on the ex-hubby and his new wife. Not that she's new now, of course. Cass might be wreaking revenge. I mean, I know we weren't exactly Romeo and Juliet, but it's like I thrust him into a kind of purgatory. Sure they may still have sex—fortunately I'm no longer privy to that—but she nags him within an inch of his life. I can hear them from my house. All the time. She's a perfectionist; he has to live up.

And he puts up with it. Bizarre stuff. I'd hate me too for releasing him to that.

And her? Well, I call her the Nagging Hag, or NagHag for short, although she's five years younger than me and as sexy as all get out. Luscious, thick blond hair. I'm not actually sure it's real. I mean can you really grow hair that luscious and thick in your thirties? And her legs, well it's like they forgot to put a torso in and just let them ride all the way to her breasts. They're long, long, long! She's a stunner, a mean, husband-stealing cow, but a stunner nonetheless. *And* she knows it. Makes him pay for it on a daily basis. She never seems to shut up. I can hear her from across the street: Natter, natter, natter, nag, nag, nag.

It's like he'd scored the perfect parking spot and now he has to keep feeding the meter, over and over. It must be exhausting. Depleting. Boring even.

So maybe he hates me for kicking him out, maybe he still holds a grudge?

I don't know, sounds a bit weak, but we're trying to keep an open mind, remember?

Then of course there's NagHag herself. Maybe Cass's second wife loathes me with a vengeance. Yes, they did make it official after a few years, and they even invited me to the wedding would you believe? Of course I didn't go, but I did let Bob tag along, if only so I could get the goss. He didn't have much to say. Bride looked "all right," Dad was "okay," food was "not bad." It's a wonder men ever become writers, they have so little to say.

Maybe NagHag feels she could have done better and I have somehow thrust a loser into her life. But again, I doubt it. I mean, she can always boot him out as I have done. Or better yet, shove a knife through *his* heart.

I'm really stuck on the knife, aren't I? There's something to be said for that. I mean, I want you to keep an open mind, but you gotta wonder why I keep coming back to the knife. It certainly felt like one before most of my senses did a runner. And what else is going to slice through your back ribs and into a heart so cleanly? Surely a pair of scissors would be too short, an axe too messy, a metal bar too fat to leave such a clean cut?

Okay, enough of the family soap opera. Let's get back to the facts shall we, or we might just run out of time. Granny is still waving me over, a warm "she'll be right" smile on her face. I know what she's doing; I'm not falling for it. She's trying to help me into the never-never, but she can bloody well back off.

Not now, Granny, I want to tell her. *I'm not ready yet!*

CHAPTER 2

Here's how my murder went down.

This morning, I awoke groggy but alive. I'd taken a sleeping pill last night, a Stilnox, on account of the fact that I hated the way my life was turning out. And I'm not talking about Cass and NagHag. We'll get into that later.

I shuffled along the hall, banged loudly on Bob's door to wake him up, then continued shuffling down to the kitchen to pop the kettle on. It was Sunday, but it was our little ritual. I woke him up around nine-ish, he pretended to ignore me, then always joined me for breaky soon after.

But not this morning, at least not straight away.

For fifteen minutes or so I tapped my tatty fingernails on the kitchen table waiting for Bob to materialise, staring up at the beaming ceiling light and thinking nothing more than, "Gee, I wonder what idiot left that on last night?"

I flicked it off just as Bob appeared, hair dishevelled, a tense look on his face. I guess he's turning into a teenager and wants to sleep in. Well, sorry bucko, not on my watch. At least he made an effort to get dressed, although wearing the same gear you wore yesterday doesn't quite count.

I didn't mention the stinky T-shirt or the sloppy timekeeping, said simply, "Toast, darl'?"

He nodded.

I didn't know if this meant he was now officially talking to me (because we'd had a tiff, if you must know), so I said, "Is that a 'Yes please, Mum, I love you so much'?"

He stared at me, hard. I knew I was pushing him, but I'd had enough of the silent treatment. I'd been getting it all week.

He nodded again, more warily this time.

Then I said five simple words I wish I had never said. They're so heinous I can't even repeat them. Not yet. Just take my word for it; they were not pretty.

Thunderstruck, Bob stared at me speechless for many seconds, then ranted for about two minutes (again please don't make me repeat what he said, not yet, not while I'm still feeling a little tender) before turning and storming from the kitchen, slamming the door on his way out.

I stared at the swinging door for several seconds. I'd forgotten we even had a kitchen door. It's almost never closed. I wanted to thrust it open again and shout at him to get back here pronto!

Oh how I wish I had. Foolishly I didn't. I simply turned to the toaster and started making toast.

Ten minutes later, I was still making toast, even though I was no longer hungry and Bob had not returned. I said I'd make him toast, and I would jolly well make him toast. And so I made sixteen slices. I just couldn't stop. I watched them brown, pulled them out, then put another two slices in. Maybe I wanted there to be plenty when he came back. Maybe I had finally flipped, who knows? I never got a chance to dissect that because I was just reaching into the freezer to pull out another loaf when the killer struck.

The knife—surely it was a knife?—pierced my back so easily it just kind of slipped in and out as though through silk, and I did feel the pain, just briefly, before I smacked into the floor.

And while I didn't see the culprit and can't imagine why my son would kill me over a few horrible words (I will tell you what they were, just give me a sec), I did see something that gave me pause for thought before I slipped off this mortal coil.

I saw a set of feet, well, shoes actually—black Converse sneakers, the exact same pair my son has. Oh, and I thought I heard a gasp that sounded a lot like him.

Then everything went black.

CHAPTER 3

Can you see now why I think my son might have done it? Can you understand my anguish? Perhaps, to understand better, we need to take a look at the prime suspect.

Bob.

He's tall for his age, a little lanky, with puddle-brown eyes, a splatter of freckles on his nose, and a sharp hairdo. He has a thing for Barcelona, a Spanish football team I assume, and fronts up to our local hairdresser, a lovely lady called Cheyzene, with a scrapbook full of magazine clippings and the words, "Please make it look just like that."

Cheyzene just smiles knowingly and sets to work. She knows what she's doing; it's the same for all the boys in the 'hood: they all seem devoted to the same team, all wear the same ugly maroon jersey every chance they get. I mean, really? Is there only one team in the entire league?

He's a popular kid, my Bob, judging by the constant greetings he gets as we wander the supermarket and the hordes of kids who hang out on our road, half on their bikes, half on skateboards, trying to steal him away. Has a pretty sweet temperament, all things considered. Rarely raises his voice to me. Doesn't *act* like a psychopath, if that's what you're wondering.

As for motive? Well, what can I say? Bob grew up with a mother who adored him and a father who lives across the road and makes love staring back at his old house. Is that so odd? Maybe it is, but you wouldn't kill because of it, right?

How about this then: Bob turned thirteen yesterday. Yep, big, big day—he's officially a teenager! Woo-hoo! Except I refused to let him have a birthday party on account of the fact that I'd busted him kissing some hussy in the local park the week before. Or rather, I hadn't busted him, I'd entrusted him to his best mate's mum, a woman called Junnifer. Well, Jennifer Cloak is her actual name, but she has airs and graces that one and a very odd way of pronouncing her rather common name. I like to call her Jenny, and it really gets her goat.

"Oh Lulu, darling, it's Junnifer if you don't mind. Jenny's not really my style."

"No worries, Jenny," I'd reply, then slap my palm to my forehead and say, "Oops, sorry, did it again!" Then I'd call her Jenny for the rest of the conversation. Eventually she would give up, although every now and then she'd give it another whirl. She failed each and every time, and I would go back to calling her Jenny all over again.

So anyway, Junnifer (I like to use her full name when she's not listening) had custody of my son last Friday night, primarily because it kept her maniacal son Sebastian entertained. I know the way these things work. No one ever invites a twelve-year-old boy over for the pure pleasure of his company. He had a job to do and that was to entertain her spoiled progeny. Except, that night, she boasted as she watched Bob slip into the back seat of her stinky, new black BMW beside "Seb", she was taking them to a film night at the local hall. I live in a small, regional town, did I tell you that much?

And by all accounts, she did take them to the hall. She just didn't bother hanging around. Probably had silverware to polish.

So what did they do? They did what all the other ratbags in the village do, they scooted out the back door and congregated down behind the hall in the local "park," a term I use advisedly because it's really just a muddy, overgrown patch of earth with a rusty swing and a rotting wooden hutch they call a tree house. Why, I don't know. It's not actually in a tree, and it's the size of a large dog kennel, but there you have it.

Anyway, that's where the aforementioned crime occurred. Not my murder, we're not there yet. I'm talking about the hussy wench who snogged my son. My as-yet-to-turn-thirteen son, I might add. Still a tween, not even a teen. Waaaay too young to lock lips with anyone, let alone tongues inside a rotting hutch. But that's exactly what happened, and I know this because I heard about it in great, florid detail the following morning from two tweenie girls who were beyond excited by the whole affair.

Tweenie girls. *Shudder.*

No offence if you have one, but I have very little patience for that lot let me tell you that. I mean, sure, they can hold a conversation, make their beds in the morning, and they don't stink out the house the second they remove their sneakers. I get it. They're perfect. But they're also so virtuous and bossy and *smug.* You wouldn't want to live with one, let's put it that way.

"Bob hooked up with Henrietta!" Yana told me the second I stepped into the corner shop, which is a sun-scorched twelve-minute stroll from my house and rarely worth the effort. Yana's dad ran the place, and Yana could usually be found behind the counter stuffing her face with free gummy bears or loitering just outside the front door, bored to her pudgy eyeballs.

"Sorry? What?" I replied.

"They were having sex!" came the shrill tones of another tweenie girl, a friend of Yana's I suspect. Half her size and twice as thick.

"Oh don't be silly!" Yana had turned on her friend. "They were just making out. That's not sex."

"Yuh it is."

"Nuh-uh! Sex is when a guy puts his—"

"When did this happen?" I demanded, not interested in a reproduction lesson from eleven-year-olds at ten in the morning while standing in a local store clutching a two-litre bottle of pasteurized milk.

"Last night, in the park," she replied, smirking so much her beady little eyes got lost in rolls of cheek fat.

"They were *sexing*," persisted the other one. The one I now wanted to smack across the head with my milk bottle.

"That's not *sexing*, Eloise." Pause for eye roll. "That's just making out. You're sooooooo juvenile!" Like she was the model of maturity.

The whole time Yana's dad was watching, also smirking behind the counter. At no point did he think to pull his daughter up, ask her to pull her head in. Instead, he gave me a "Don't you just love kids?" look, and now it was *his* head I wanted to smack in.

I paid for the milk and got the hell out of there, not sure whether I was angrier with him for looking so delighted by the whole exchange or Yana for spreading malicious gossip about my son and that hussy.

A few hours later, when Bob got home from his "sleepover"—again, we need to use quotation marks there, you can bet very little sleep was had what with all the brutal, blood-drenched PlayStation games young Sebastian is spoiled rotten with—I bailed him up. Well, kind of.

"So how was the film at the hall last night?"

He shrugged, opened the fridge door, and stared vacantly inside. "All right."

"What was it about?"

"Dunno. Something."

"Who was starring in it?"

"Dunno. Someone."

"Any snogging going on?"

He turned from the fridge door and looked at me. "Huh?"

"Just wondering, anybody do any kissing? You know, in the movie or maybe later on?"

He looked like I'd flipped, didn't have the good grace to blush, just turned back to the fridge and reached for a tub of yoghurt. "Dunno. Nah, don't think so."

"Right," I said. "Anything you want to tell me then?"

He ripped the lid off his yoghurt and shrugged again. "Nope." He began to lick the top clean. It's a pet hate of mine. I mean, is there not enough in the tub to keep you happy? If not, just open another tub.

"Fine," I said, then added, "The party's off."

"What?"

"You heard me, your thirteenth birthday party is cancelled. Kaput."

All hell broke loose then, of course. You see, boys are men of few words until it pleases them, then you can't shut the buggers up.

"What? Nooo! It can't be cancelled! You said I could have a sleepover party. You said it ages ago. You promised! You promised on your grandma's life! You said I could have twelve mates and we'd toast marshmallows and… and you promised. I've been planning it *all* year, I've got it all sorted, everyone's really excited! So it's happening, okay? It's happening!"

I let him get through the first stage of grieving—denial. Then waited while the second stage kicked in. Anger.

"Well, you can bloody well drop dead because there's no way I'm telling everyone they can't come. You can't do that, Mum. It's the kinda shit you do to me all the time! You make my life miserable. I hate you, I hate you, I *hate* you!"

When that didn't cut the mustard, he tried bargaining. "Come on, Mum, please? *Pleeeeease?*"

I shook my head. "Sorry, no, I've changed my mind."

"But… but you can't do that!"

"Why not?"

"Because you just can't. You gave your word. You can't break your word!"

"Oh but you can?"

He looked perplexed, so I helped him out. "Last night you gave me your word you were going to quietly sit in the local hall and watch a movie with Sebastian. That's what you said you were going to do, but you broke your word."

"Ah, no, Mum. I never actually *said* that."

I held up a finger. "Ah yes, but you *inferred* it. By agreeing to accompany Sebastian to a film at the hall, the inference—the contract between us (my finger was now pointing from him to me and back again)—was that you would stay inside the hall watching said film. But you did not. (Finger was now pointing straight at his head.) You slipped out the back and had your merry way with that girl."

As my finger now did a dirty dance in the air, he looked stunned.

"But… but…"

Bam! I got you there! I dropped my hand, smiled smugly, and walked out of the kitchen and up to my bedroom where I shut the door. Okay, that was an unfair move—not cancelling the party, that was justified, he shouldn't be snogging girls in rotting hutches, especially girls that were due to show up to his sleepover party in just a week's time. No, I was hitting below the belt by storming into my bedroom. It's kind of like my "out of bounds."

Bob never enters my bedroom and vice versa. Not since he decided at the age of nine that sleeping anywhere near me was a repulsive thought. These days we're less "peas in a pod" and more "two ships passing in the night." So my bedroom has become sacred territory now, the perfect bunker when we're getting on each other's nerves. He never crosses the threshold, and I never ask him to. And I certainly never go into his room, at least not while he's around. So I escaped to my bedroom and forced the issue to drop.

But he didn't let it drop. He sulked for the full week and then all day yesterday, on his birthday. He ignored the cake I'd baked him, too, until the thick chocolate icing got the better of him and I caught him sneaking a slice.

But this is not the reason I think he killed me even though he did say the actual words, "Well you can drop dead." You did catch that, right? Well, you need to know I really don't think my son would slay me over a disappointing birthday.

I think he killed me because the very next day (i.e. this morning, are you keeping up?), I told him to pack up and piss off.

CHAPTER 4

Okay, so I didn't use those words exactly, and I didn't mean that Bob had to go live on the cold, hard streets, if that's what you're thinking. Come *on*, I might be tough, but I'm no monster! He's thirteen for goodness' sake. He just had to cross the road and live with his dad for a bit. While I regret those words now, it's not quite child abuse, is it? Besides, I had good cause. Snogging girls wasn't what forced my hand; that was just the final straw.

Bob was busted smoking a cigarette last month. I feel like he's on the slippery slope to heroin addiction and homelessness. Did I mention he'd only just turned thirteen? He's a baby for crying out loud. Way too young to be mucking around with tongues and tobacco. At the very least he really has to learn, there are no secrets in a small town, everybody knows everybody's business. I heard about the smokes from another girl, an older one, this one called Fran and usually far too terrified of me to say boo. But I guess she was determined to save Bob from himself, so had found the courage to approach me at the school bus stop one day and, chewing on a tight, flaxen plait, whispered, "I saw Bobby smoke a cigarette yesterday. It's really bad for his health. Just sayin'."

That was all she had to say.

That afternoon, over a cup of coffee, I told Cass he had to take charge of his son.

"He's looking for some boundaries, some discipline.

I'm doing more than enough; it's time for you to step up. He's yours when he turns thirteen."

I know now, in retrospect—which is pretty much all you have left when you're dead—that I would never have sent him to live with his dad. I'd miss him too much. It didn't stop me from threatening to though. It didn't stop me from saying those five heinous words just minutes before I was murdered.

Pack. Up. You're. Moving. Out.

At first he didn't believe me, so I repeated myself and watched as his face deflated.

Eventually he found his tongue, as I knew he would. "What! Why?"

"I'm getting no respect around here. It's time you lived with your father."

He stared at me bug-eyed. "But… but *why?*"

"Because I love you and I think it's for the best."

"For the *best?* For the best! What the…!"

And off he went, verbose again after seven days of silence, shouting stuff about how hideous his half sisters were and how they all hated him and I must too if I was banishing him to "that house" and how could I possibly do this to him and he hated me now more than he ever thought possible. You get the drift. His voice was louder than usual, so I guess I really got under his skin this time.

"I always defend you," he continued. "I always do, but she's so right about you—you are a bitch!" He slapped a hand to his mouth, clearly as shocked by the words as I was, but I chose not to react.

Instead, I said simply, "Who's that, dear?" knowing full well he meant NagHag. Who else would slander me to my own child?

But he was shaking his head angrily again and stormed out of the room, slamming the kitchen door closed as he went.

You know what happens next.

Whether I would have gone through with my threat is now, frankly, irrelevant. My death has sentenced Bob to "that house" anyway, living with that perfect-looking woman and her two perfect girls.

Did I mention they have a couple of tweenie girls? Now you can understand my animosity. It's not personal, really. It's just that they're so nauseatingly perfect. I come home sometimes and find they've all placed their perfect little joggers in perfect little rows just outside their front door, right next to their perfect pink bikes that are also rust-free and perfectly in place. Then I glance at my own front veranda and see a twisted mishmash of muddy shoes, hole-riddled socks, Bob's beaten-up old bike on its side, half the spokes missing, the tires flat. You understand now?

As I say, I don't know whether I really would have forced Bob to live with that mob if I'd lived to see the day out, but my death has certainly made it inevitable. So it makes no sense, then, that Bob would slaughter me to avoid moving out.

Now he has no choice.

Can you see now why I'm in a muddle?

CHAPTER 5

So now you have the background, what little of it I have time to share. Now you need to watch closely as a policeman arrives precisely six minutes after my murder. Not because Bob has dialled 000—he hasn't. He's holed up in his bedroom, no doubt sulking about his crappy life and wondering how long he can maintain the charade before he comes down and has his toast. Hunger has always undermined his sulks. I think it might be a boy thing. I often overhear other mothers say their daughters can string a sulk out for weeks, months, sometimes even years. Bob doesn't have the stamina for that.

The doorbell rings and rings, and eventually he shuffles out of his room, curiosity overriding crankiness. Not curiosity over who's at the door, mind you, but curiosity as to why I haven't answered it. I normally leap upon the door. I don't have a lot of friends, so it's always a major revelation when someone shows up.

"Mum, someone at the door!" he calls out as he plods down the stairs and past the kitchen, the door still closed, thankfully. He heads towards the front of the house, opens the door, steps back a little as he spots the uniformed officer with the stern expression on his face.

"Ya mum here, mate?"

"Oh, yeah, sure," Bob says, still staring at the copper as he yells, his face slightly angled towards the kitchen. "Muuum! Policeman here to see you!"

He continues ogling the uniformed officer for a few minutes as though he's quite impressed that a man in uniform has come to his door, then calls again.

When I don't magically appear, he frowns and says, "Just a sec."

Leaving the copper on the doorstep, he steps towards the kitchen and swings the door wide open, and that's when he sees me, spread-eagled on the floor.

"Mum?" he asks, his voice curious as he bends down towards me, then catching sight of the blood on my back, I hear his breath catch and a guttural moan come out from somewhere deep inside. It makes him sound like a man.

"Muuuuum!" he cries, and I think my heart will break all over again.

Bob is wailing now, shoving my shoulder over and over as if trying to wake me, and the policeman comes running in, tries to pull my son back, but he's not letting go.

All of this sounds good right? Sounds like an innocent child discovering his murdered mother, shocked and upset. So why did I see his shoes just as I was killed? How do the two line up?

I don't know, that's where you come in. You need to sort truth from fiction, reality from a theatrical son. Did I mention he's a half-decent actor? Got the drama prize last semester. I mean, sure, it's only a small regional school and it's not exactly an Academy Award, but there are plenty of drama queens in his composite class (see aforementioned notes on Yana and Eloise), so it's not to be sneezed at.

Is Bob acting now? Or is he genuinely distraught? I can tell you, if it's the former, he would give O. J. Simpson a run for his money.

Copper manages to pull my sobbing son away and checks my pulse. Of course he finds nothing. I even hear him sigh. He doesn't know me, but he's sad and I'm glad of it. You want your death to upset people. Nobody wants their wake to be too much fun.

The copper pulls out his mobile phone and speaks anxiously into it, calling for backup and an ambulance. Really, why bother with all that? I'm gone for good, no amount of "Charging… Five hundred… Clear!" is going to change that.

Copper then looks around as though it's only just occurred to him that I'm not only dead, I've been murdered. I mean, unless I had twisty arms that could reach behind and stab my own back, some bugger did this, and he might still be in the house. Curious copper doesn't think to point the finger at Bob initially, and I am glad of it. I mean, who would? The boy is just thirteen, and he's put on a pretty good crying act.

Bob is now standing by the kitchen door, propping it open, his head turned away from me but unable to peel his eyes off. Is he in shock or is he just checking to make sure I don't spring back to life?

I know I need to be more objective. I know I need to stop steering you towards my beloved boy, but I have to be honest and I have to tell you what I see, and this is it: My son standing by the kitchen door, looking both distraught and a little too worried for his own good. And it worries me.

Copper has my son by the arm now and is dragging him into the living room where the television is on. Now that's even weirder than the kitchen light. Why would the telly be on at 9.35 in the morning, before either of us has entered the lounge room? I never turned it on. Did Bob? I doubt it. He was in his bedroom, sulking remember? *Or was he?* I have to wonder now.

The copper is asking Bob a series of questions. Bob is not responding.

"Do you know what happened?"

"Did you see anyone?"

"Did you touch anything?"

A siren wails far off and then another one, and I know the troops are coming and my son is up shit creek. He's the only one in the house, how can they *not* pin this on him? Please help me find him a paddle.

CHAPTER 6

Tell me quickly: Where could the murder weapon be? I can't see it. Copper seems to be aware of this, too, and leaves Bob sitting on the lounge, pale and now sobbing, while he walks almost gingerly back into the kitchen, locating the small plastic thingie that holds that door open. He secures it in place, then glances quickly down at me, just checking perhaps that I am still lying there in my black briefs, as frozen as the loaf of bread beside me.

I've never been the sexy lingerie type. Perhaps that's where I went wrong with Cass. I see the catalogues, I wander past those sparkly stores with their slutty mannequins, and I get it. The stuff is gorgeous, provocative, glamorous. But it also looks bloody uncomfortable. I know that stuff would ride right up, the cleavage-inducing wires poke right in. I just don't have the patience for that kind of nonsense. Or I didn't. Now lying in my boring Bonds undies, I wish I had.

Fortunately, copper doesn't seem too nonplussed. He looks around again, steps towards the sink, looks in there too. Sees nothing, unless you count the dusting of charcoal I recently scraped off some of the toast. He steps towards the back door of the kitchen, which is slightly ajar.

Aha! There's another clue, and this one looks good for my Bob. That definitely wasn't open this morning; I would have noticed that for sure. I never opened it. I was too busy making toast. And Bob was in his room. So why is it ajar? Surely that proves someone else did it.

Doesn't it?

Using his sleeve to cover his hands, copper (clearly no idiot) pulls the door wider and leans out. He looks down the mouldy cement steps to our dreary backyard. It's better than the local park but only by a few pot plants. I'm not much of a gardener, never was. That was Cass's territory, or at least it was for the short time we lived together in faux domestic bliss.

There's a loud banging on the front door now, and copper steps back into the kitchen, gives me another glance—does he really think I might vanish?—then rushes for the front door and unlocks it. It locks automatically from inside, in case you were wondering, and I think you should be if you want to solve this thing.

So that's when the real commotion starts. I watch it all from a kind of suspended universe. As I said before, I'm not simply floating above, like they say in books, but I'm not lying on that floor either. I'm not really sure where I am, to be honest, but let's not worry about that for now.

A fleet of cop cars have arrived, and four more officers, all in uniform, are now standing at the open door of the kitchen staring at me. They seem genuinely interested in checking out my corpse. I guess I can't blame them. It is a curious sight. How often do *you* get to check out a dead woman lying in a pool of blood on her kitchen linoleum, piles and piles of cold toast above her on the bench?

"What's with all the bread?" some bright spark ventures, and they all peel their eyes from my corpse to survey the scene. Nobody answers. They do not know. How could they? *Just another mad housewife* they probably think, although their thoughts are not open to me.

Now that is strange. I always thought death would enable the sixth sense. How disappointing.

Anyway, soon someone in a different uniform squeezes past them, followed by another. Must be the paramedics.

One of them, the smaller, female one, methodically takes my pulse, pulls my eyelids back, and shines a torch into my pupils and then declares the bleeding obvious to no one in particular.

"She's deceased."

It's like a load has lifted, and I feel a certain brightness enter the house. I can tell at least two of the cops are happy about this. Not the one who found me, mind, he still seems a bit sad, which is just lovely, but the other two, a fat one with a goatee and a thinner one with a badly receding hairline. They're almost twitching with joy.

"Better alert Homicide," the balding one says and steps out of the kitchen and back to the front door, a jig in his step. It's like he's been waiting his whole career to say that.

"What happened?" Goatee Guy asks the first copper, the sad one.

He blushes. "I don't know! I just came to serve the lady an AVO. She was already dead."

"An Apprehended Violence Order?" he says, which is very helpful of him because for a moment there I wasn't sure what that meant. "Wow," Goatee Guy continues, "so the brutal bastard got to her first, hey?"

He does a little tut-tut, and First Copper looks confused for a second, then shakes his head.

"Nah, mate, the restraining order was taken out against *her*. She was the perpetrator."

Now Goatee Guy looks confused and scratches at his prickly beard.

"Wow, okay, that's odd. Maybe he did it in self-defence then. Who took it out? Hubby? Boyfriend? An ex?" He clearly has aspirations to be a detective, that one.

"Some chick," says the other cop.

That forces the goatee into a smile. "You serious?"

First Cop nods solemnly.

Goatee Guy chews on that for a bit. "That the son in there?"

They both lean a little so they can see across the

corridor and into the living room where Bob is seated, head in his hands. I wish one of them would go in and give him a cuddle. They lean back.

"Yep, was as shocked as I was."

"He the only one home?"

"Oh shit," the first copper says, darts into the living room, and says to my son, "Anyone else here? Your dad? Any siblings?"

Bob doesn't move his head from his hands as he shakes his head no.

Clearly not prepared to take his word for it, both coppers are now rushing through the house, thrusting open cupboards, checking under beds. They find nothing, of course, no shocked baby sister or blood-dripping de facto cowering behind the shower curtain. But Goatee Guy does stop to check out my wardrobe for a little too long. I wonder if he has a thing for women's clothing and wonder why he bothers. My dresses are about as thrilling as my lingerie. I half expect him to start fossicking through my underwear drawer.

He doesn't though, just returns to the kitchen where First Copper has a look of utter relief on his face. Apart from the backyard, he hadn't thought to look beyond the kitchen sink. His boss would probably have his balls for breakfast if he knew that. I'm no copper, let's face it, but it's gotta be Policing 101—call the ambo, secure the scene and, oh yeah, look for the culprit.

With cops like these clowns, I'm really glad you've come along for the ride.

CHAPTER 7

The momentum is starting to build. Soon after the paramedics depart, also wearing confronting looks of relief, a steady stream of crime-scene heroes begins to fill the house. I guess some are with Forensics, some with the Homicide Squad, I can't tell exactly as they all seem to know each other and no one bothers with introductions, unhelpful as that is. I hear a Johnno, a Babe, a Tandy Darlin', and a You Fat Bastard. At no point, at least not in the first ten minutes or so, does anyone stop to see how my son is doing, and I am livid.

Wake up, people! There's a child in there, shaking his little heart out!

When a guy called Chief arrives, I quickly realise why they've left Bob unattended. The top dog wants to sniff him out before a kindly relative sticks a muzzle on him or demands he is read his rights. Chief takes a cursory look at the body, I mean me, then asks, "So where is he?"

First Cop nods his head towards the living room, and Chief wanders in and sits across from my son in the guest armchair, the one I try not to use lest I wear it out.

Why did I do that? Why deny myself a really comfy armchair every day for thirteen years on the off-chance the Queen will come to visit or, worse, a homicide detective who's about to incriminate my son? Now I wish I could go back and jump muddy footprints all over the bloody thing.

"I'm the lead detective, Bob. You want to tell me what

happened here?" Chief is asking, and Bob looks up from his hands, dazed and glassy-eyed.

"Huh?"

"Do you want to tell me what happened to your mum?"

Now Bob just blinks back.

Oh Bob, I think, don't turn into Mute Boy now. Be verbose, give them details, tell them you were in your bedroom the whole time! Or if you have to, channel your inner O. J. But he doesn't seem to be capable of anything.

Chief asks where he was when it happened, and he mumbles, "Huh?"

Chief asks if he knows what happened to me, if he saw anyone, if he has any idea what's going on, and all the while Bob stares at him stunned and unable to say a thing beyond the word "Huh." If I never hear that word again, I'll be the happiest woman alive. I mean dead. I want to weep, but my tear ducts are no longer functioning.

Then something very strange happens. Out of nowhere Junnifer appears.

"Oh you poor, poor darling!" she cries, sweeping into the lounge room and straight to my son who stands, steps towards her and into her arms.

I should be relieved. I said he needed a cuddle, but not Jenny, please God, anyone but Junnifer!

She is patting my son's back and answering Chief's questions very calmly, very politely. "Yes, I'm a very good family friend."

Na-uh! I want to scream. She's just the snotty-nosed mother of my son's wayward mate.

"Yes, I was just driving past. I saw the cars. I wondered what had happened."

I bet you did, you gossipy cow! And what do you mean you were just driving past? I live in the quiet end of town. No reason to come anywhere near my house unless Sebastian has a play date, which he doesn't, or wants a lift to the old skate park nearby, which he never does.

"No, the officer outside told me what happened." She choked back a sob. "Poor, poor Lulu. I mean, she could be, well, *trying*, but she didn't deserve that!"

Ah, hello? You're saying that in my son's arms. He appears to stiffen at this, but perhaps I'm just wishful projecting. In any case, he soon untangles himself from her, and before he can drop back onto the couch, she is leading him out of the living room and through the front door but not before taking a sneaky peek herself towards my lifeless body, which is still lying on the kitchen floor in all its bloody glory. I'm not sure if I'm just imagining things, but I would swear on my grandmother's life—hell, my own life I suppose—that she has a glimmer of relief in her eyes.

Chief doesn't attempt to stop either of them from leaving the house, and I hate her and love her now in equal measure. Good, I think, get him out of there. But stop hugging him like he's your son.

My body's not cold yet, baby. Besides, you don't get first dibs.

As they hobble across the road, past a few curious neighbours, in the direction of Cass's house, I notice the copper with the receding hairline is already there, banging on my ex-husband's front door like there's no tomorrow. Someone must have finally put two and two together, but they've come up stumps. There is no answer from inside, and I have to wonder why.

It's Sunday morning, and Cass is usually in there somewhere, lurking about, waiting for trophy wife to come home from soccer. Yes, her girls do play soccer, and she trains at least one of them while he stays home and waits it out. Did I mention he was useless?

I know what you're thinking: Why don't I just look inside Cass's house and see if the useless git is scrubbing blood from his fingernails as we speak? Well, it's like I said. For some reason I can't explain, I can't see into every room or every house. I can't see into Bob's bedroom, for instance, and I can't see into the bathroom with the adjoining toilet, although I'm not sure that's such a bad thing. And I certainly can't see into Cass and NagHag's overly renovated hovel.

It's all very bizarre, but let's try to focus on what I can see, okay?

I can see Junnifer has walked my son onto the front veranda and helped him into one of the perfectly painted wicker chairs out the front of the house. Again I am grateful for that. The gathering vultures, I mean *voyeurs*, are staring towards my house, so it feels safer over there, and no one pays him much notice. Maybe Junnifer's not so bad.

Hell, she's not the one with a restraining order out against her, is she?

About that…

CHAPTER 8

It's time to address the elephant in the room. I know you took note of that restraining order; it's probably all you can think about. So let's get this over and done with, shall we, so we can get back to the important stuff? I might have been a devoted mum, but I was a pretty ordinary employee, the worst kind, in fact.

I slept with my married boss.

There, I said it. I'm not proud of it, if that helps. I bitterly regret the whole debacle, but in my defence, I have to say he took advantage of a woman at her most vulnerable.

His name is Todd Karlouis. Your classic sleazy boss cliché: thinning on top, widening around the middle, ogling anything in a skirt.

I'd become achingly lonely since Cass moved out, and recently, as Bob spent more time with mates like Sebastian and that hussy Henrietta, the loneliness had become acute. Bob was growing away from me, and it hurt. I guess that's why I was pushing him away. Then I had no one to blame but myself.

Sleazebag Todd (aka Toadface) sensed my desperation and abused it, luring me into an equally sleazy tryst, but then his wife found out and threatened to kill me—oh, there's another suspect, yay!—and so I threatened to kill her back. I wasn't serious, but I might have said something like, "Not if I kill you first."

Juvenile, I know, but who knew she'd take it literally and slap me with an Apprehended Violence Order? I gather it's to ensure I don't go within a something-kilometre radius. Or at least I think that's what First Copper was wielding when he knocked on my door this morning.

Unless somebody else thinks I'm out to get them? Hmmm. I should think about that.

In any case, Mrs Karlouis needn't have bothered. Not only did Toadface throw me out on my arse, I swore off men forever. Take it from me, jealous wifey didn't have to kill me. I would have stabbed my own back if I were forced to go back to that creep.

I cleaned holiday rentals for a living, did I tell you that? Was quite good at my job, I might add, before I got the boot. Quite popular with the other staffers too (the cleaners, the receptionist, the woman who did accounts); they all delighted in my wicked sense of humour and total lack of respect for authority. Fat lot of good that did me. None of them ever wanted to pursue a friendship outside of work. It's like they found me hilarious on the job but didn't want to share my jokes later over cheeky Chardies at the local pub.

I didn't take it personally. I've had that effect on others my whole life. People always find me mildly amusing, occasionally shocking, sort of like a naughty stand-up comic or a clown. Great fun for a bit, but you'd never invite one back to your house, right?

I work for a company called Yeah BnB. I know, Airbnb must be shittin' itself. It's a dinky-di little business that Todd started about five years back to help local landlords rent out their spare bedrooms, granny flats, dank corners... you get the drift. Toadface ran the operation from a few creaky computers in a shabby little office in town, and I spent half my time prepping the homes for guests (cleaning, fresh sheeting, general tszujing up) and the other half hanging at headquarters batting away Todd's advances.

But he was persistent.

I suspect that's why the slimeball employed me in the first place. Not because I was handy with a mop, but because he clocked me as a potential conquest, a "desperate and dateless" from the moment we met, and I was sorry I did not disappoint.

It seemed to me, the more I resisted, the more he tried it on, and eventually I couldn't find the will to say no. Or perhaps I was worried about my job. If I didn't put out at some stage, would he put me out to pasture? Jobs are few and far between in this regional town. I couldn't risk it. Yes, I can see the irony—it cost me my job regardless.

So one thing led to another, and we ended up in the sack. Well, the supplies shed if you must know, and now I had his feral wife taking restraining orders out against me like it was all *my* fault.

Still, there is a silver lining. That AVO brought the cop to my door this morning and eased the burden for Bob of finding my lifeless body. I wonder if Curious Copper hadn't knocked, what would have happened (assuming Bob didn't do it, of course). Would starvation eventually have forced him out of his sulk and back to the kitchen to find me? Would he have known what to do? He might have compromised any potential evidence. He might have been foolish enough to close that back door, switch off that telly.

See these are the clues you need to focus on, and fast. Because that blasted light is intensifying, and Gran no longer looks happy, she looks ready to have another coronary. Did you know she died of a heart attack? In her sleep? At age eighty-nine? How ideal is that? No wonder she thinks I should "go gentle into that good night." It's all very well for her; she had no unfinished business. She must have been gagging for it by the time the tunnel light finally flickered on.

So I'm ignoring her frantically waving arms and trying to concentrate on the crime scene, which is now being manned by a woman, a uniformed officer who has a look of complete and utter boredom on her acne-splattered face.

I don't think it's boring at all! Even the simple blue-and-white police tape sends ripples of excitement through the growing throng, and I don't blame them. At some stage, they taped up my entire property, from the cobwebbed letterbox to the garage on one side and my rickety old fence on the other. Suddenly it all looks very important.

The crowd, now swollen to at least twenty, are standing just beyond the tape, as though it might electrocute them. It's amazing how humans obey that flimsy plastic barrier. Perhaps we should all string it up at night to propel burglars and molesters. Or knife-wielding types, perhaps? Again with the irony.

It's a motley crew out there watching the proceedings, some busybody neighbours like old Mrs Oliver who lives next door to Cass, others I don't recognise, but there is one face in the crowd that gives me pause for thought. Hell, it gives me cause for delight. It's Sarah Burleigh from two blocks down, and she would make a really terrific suspect.

CHAPTER 9

I read somewhere that one in one hundred people are certified psychopaths. According to the experts, every suburb/office block/church group has one. Our resident psychopath is Sarah Burleigh, one very scary mother. And I mean that quite literally. Sarah also happens to be the mother of Henrietta, the little hussy who dared to steal my son's first kiss. You can see now why I was so aghast at Bob swapping saliva with that child. I don't just hate that he betrayed my trust, I hate that he did so with the offspring of a madwoman.

What if Psycho Sarah took issue with my son shoving his tongue down her daughter's throat? Would she begin one of her notorious vendettas against us? I've seen her vendettas in action. The sheer power of her hatred is inspiring, can force entire families out of the neighbourhood, which has happened. Twice.

The last one was a lovely hippy couple who had a penchant for smoking pot in their backyard. Sure, you could smell it a mile off, but you couldn't see them and no one really cared. Except for Sarah. She marched over there one day, mentioned "decent neighbourhood" and "local police," and before you know it, the hippies had packed up their Kombi and pissed off.

She's been known to steer her muddy 4WD towards people she doesn't like, toppling one poor guy off his bicycle, causing another to dive into the nearest bush.

I've even witnessed her trip up an old bloke. I kid you not. He'd just left the local greyhound track and was strutting down the street looking pretty proud of himself when she put out one leg and made him tumble. She never even looked back.

Why does she do all this? Who knows? It's like she's got a penchant for power, a desire to instil panic wherever she goes. And she certainly does that.

Not only is she menacing, she's the size of a house. No, make that a McMansion, one with Greek columns for arms and brick chimneys for legs. I've seen grown men cross the street to avoid impact with Sarah, and if Mike Tyson lived here, I'd give him two rounds, tops.

Yet it was her tenacious animosity that really knocked you for six. If Sarah gets the shits with you, you're screwed. Sorry, but that's the brutal truth. She was like a dog with a bone, and by dog I mean woolly mammoth. I was as in awe of it as much as I was petrified.

But you want to know what petrified me even more? What if Psycho Sarah *likes* Bob? What if she *approves* of her daughter's new boyfriend and they end up married one day and I'm suddenly related to the crazy cow? Then it's not as simple as moving suburbs. I'm stuck for life.

I shuddered at the thought then, and I shudder at it now, or I would if I had control of my limbs (which, in case you're wondering, are now being pored over by some woman in a green plastic onesie with the words "Forensic Services" on the back).

Which reminds me, my murder: What's it got to do with Henrietta and her nutjob mum? Well, they're part of the crowd that has begun to loiter on the street outside my house. Have they just arrived? Heard the goss and thought they'd check it out? Or were they in the vicinity, like Junnifer, and have just hung around?

And, more importantly, did Psycho Sarah want me dead? Did she really think that would somehow save her hussy daughter from herself?

Doesn't really add up, does it? She might be aggro, but I'm not sure Sarah has a good enough motive. All she had to do was say "Boo," and Bob and I would have packed our bags and caught the first bus out.

Still, she does have a strange satisfied look about her. Maybe she just revels in other people's tragedy. At least Henrietta has the good grace to look shocked and horrified. She's chewing mercilessly at her thumbnail, her feathery eyebrows knitted together, but she's not looking at my house, she's staring in the other direction, towards Junnifer and my son who is still hunched over in one of NagHag's crisply painted wicker chairs.

I wonder what Henrietta's thinking. I wish I knew. As I said before, I can't read people's thoughts, or if I can, I haven't yet worked out how.

Perhaps she's wondering, as I am, why Bob's dad still has not materialised.

CHAPTER 10

"Do you know where your dad is, sport?"

That's the copper with the receding hairline, who has given up hammering Cass's door down and taken to patronising my son.

Sport says nothing, so copper turns to Junnifer, who is still hanging around like yesterday's Vindaloo.

"Do you have any idea, madame, where Mr Jones might be this morning? Have you seen him around?"

Junnifer looks flummoxed suddenly. Almost outraged. "No I have not! I don't live in this street. Why would I have seen him?"

"I just thought..."

She huffs and looks away.

I don't know about you, but I'm not sure why Junnifer's in such a tizz. He was just asking. Before I can develop that thought, my attention is drawn back to the road where a gleaming white Volvo is just pulling off and into Cass's driveway.

Blond hubby stealer has arrived home, her even blonder daughters wide-eyed inside the family wagon, their faces to the glass. Brenda (that's NagHag's actual name) pulls the car to a stop just before the garage and quickly gets out, glancing first at Bob, then across the road to my house, a frown blemishing her ridiculously perfect face.

"What's going on?" she calls out to Junnifer, who rushes across and whispers something back.

Like my death is still a secret that shall remain unspoken.

Brenda places a hand to her mouth and gasps, looks almost sad, which is rather decent of her, then turns to her daughters (now, what are their names again?) who have also barrelled out of the vehicle and are now staring towards my house, more curious than concerned.

She must have told them what's happened because they mimic her reaction, hands to mouths, looks of deep sadness now popping into all four perfect blue eyes. I'm quite touched by this. Was I really expecting high-fives all round?

Brenda is now reaching for Bob, who does not jump up and hug her as he did Junnifer, and this makes me smile. Or at least it would if I still had movement of my mouth.

We might just pretend I have full control of my body if that's okay with you. It still feels like I do, in much the same way amputees feel their limbs long after they've been removed. I can't see my arms extended before me or my legs below, but I can still feel their presence. I still feel more human than spirit.

It reminds me of that Leonard Cohen lyric: "I ache in the places where I used to play."

That's how it feels to me. Perhaps it all takes a bit of getting used to.

"Where's Dad?" I hear Bob mumble, and Brenda looks to Junnifer and then to the copper who is shaking his head.

"We have tried knocking, madame. He doesn't seem to be home."

"Well that's *odd*."

Now Brenda is reaching for her house keys, unlocking her front door, calling out my husband's name, I mean, *her* husband, the one she pinched while I was breastfeeding a tiny tot. Not that I'm holding a grudge.

All three blondies disappear into the house, Bob

swallowed up in their fold. Junnifer is still standing outside. She looks around as though unsure what to do, and I want to scream, "Thanks, Jenny, but you can piss off now!"

She turns to look back towards my house and must spot someone she knows because her demeanour changes. She looks suddenly panicked and strides across the street and into the crowd. Now I see who she's glowering at. It's her son, Sebastian.

And he has black Converse sneakers on.

CHAPTER 11

Don't get too excited. You haven't solved this thing yet. I've been a bit remiss, haven't given nearly enough description of the key players. You see, Junnifer is also wearing black sneakers, so too Brenda and at least one of her girls. They may not be Converse, Nikes are more their style, but they could match the description of the last thing I saw before I blacked out. How much can we trust that? I'm not exactly in the running for fashion editor at *Vogue* (see earlier notes on my lingerie).

Oh and Psycho Sarah, who's now walking away from my house, barking into her mobile phone, she's got black shoes on, but hers are black Crocs. I told you she was psycho, right?

Why is everyone wearing black shoes today, I hear you ask? Is it just bad luck, or is it one of those annoying coincidences that mystery writers delight in? Whatever the cause, there is one player we can cross off the list. Cass has appeared—from *inside* the house, I kid you not—and there's not a stitch on his hairy, oversized toes.

Cass is wearing nothing but a pair of wrinkled shorts and a dazed look on his face. He has one arm wrapped around my son, and they are both now standing on his front veranda, watching the commotion.

I want to call out and ask, *"Where the bloody hell were you? Why didn't you answer your front door you slack arse?"*

And I have plenty more questions where those came

from, like: Why has it taken this long for you to appear? Did you not hear the freaking sirens? The crowds? *The bashing on your front door?* Have you been sleeping the whole time? Showering? Or have you been elsewhere, throwing a pair of black Converses into the nearest creek, then sneaking back into your house via the back door?

I want to know what he's been doing all morning, and why he wasn't there for our son.

I'm not the only one.

Receding Hairline has flagged down Chief, who is now striding across the street in Cass's direction. Good, maybe he'll get some answers.

Chief pulls Cass away from Bob, who takes one more heart-wrenching glance in my general direction (bless him!), then returns inside.

"What's going on over there?" Cass asks, rubbing his head as though his brain's about to explode. "What's happened to poor Lulu?"

I am touched by his tone, but I am not convinced.

"That's what we're here to find out," Chief replies. "I'm Detective Colin Chasin. I believe you're Bob's dad? You were married to the victim?"

"A million years ago, yeah." He thrusts out his hand like it's a social call. "I'm Cassowary Jones."

Chasin doesn't bat an eyelid at the loony name (he deals with pimps and drug lords; he's probably heard worse), just shakes Cass's hand and says, "Can you tell me where you've been all morning?"

"Yes, I... I was inside." Cass flutters his eyes in the direction of the house.

"The whole time, sir?"

"Yes!"

"And you didn't hear my man knocking? You didn't hear the police sirens?"

"No, I..." He sighs. "I took a Stilnox."

"A what?"

"A sleeping tablet. Was out for the count."

Oh really? He's having trouble sleeping like me. Now there's a coincidence I'd think twice about.

Chief doesn't seem to buy it either. His brow furrows, and he goes to say something when a whistle diverts his attention. There is a woman over there signalling for him to return. She is wearing a tight black suit that does little for her enormous thighs.

"Stay here," he instructs my ex. "I'll need to question you again."

Cass looks like the guy is insane. "Where am I going to go? This is where I live."

"Then you might want to answer your door next time, hey?"

Chief gives him a pointed look, then starts to leave when Cass has a sudden thought.

"Hang on, has anyone told Dot?"

Oh God. I'd forgotten all about her.

"Dot?" says the Chief.

"Dorothy Gold. Lulu's mum. She's at the old people's home, down just behind—"

"Yes, sir, we have someone with Mrs Gold now. She has agreed to identify the body."

"But I thought Bob saw…?" He can't finish that sentence.

"It's always important to get an adult to make an official identification."

"Oh, right. Of course."

He's probably wondering why they didn't ask *him*, but I am glad of it. It must mean he's a potential suspect. Good. That'll give him something to stew over. "Million years" indeed! Chief is darting back across the road, raising his eyebrows to the woman with the enormous thighs.

"What's so urgent?" he says. "I was just getting started."

"Sorry, Chief," says Thunder Thighs, not sounding one bit sorry. "But I think you're gonna wanna see this. We've found the murder weapon."

CHAPTER 12

Well, wouldn't you know it, it's a knife.

While we were being distracted by Cass's whereabouts and that silly little AVO (honestly I should never have mentioned it), the real action was happening down in the back paddock.

I live on a quarter-acre block in a sprawling green suburb that's clumped rather incongruously on one side by endless dairy cows and on the other by thick, subtropical rainforest. And between me and said forest is a muddy creek. That's where the knife was found. Not in the creek, mind, that would have been smart, but beside it, on the grassy bank. Perhaps the crim can't throw to save himself?

In any case, there's much buzz and excitement down there. It was discovered by another uniformed copper, a petite brunette with eyes like a Japanese manga girl, wide and smudged black, much like the knife she is now holding in her gloved hands.

I watch as she places it carefully into a plastic bag, as though terrified it might break, then makes her way up to the house, receiving high-fives all round. If this were a game of Aussie Rules footy, she'd be up for the Brownlow Medal.

Really, they should all head back to the locker room and take a cold shower. This ain't no winning goal. I *doubt* they'll get a perfect set of incriminating fingerprints from the knife. Not only is it covered in gunk, you don't have to be Agatha Christie to know that gloves are now *de rigueur* when stabbing someone. Only a moron would have forgotten that.

I haven't had a really good look at it myself yet, but I'm pretty sure it's the sharp one I use to chop pumpkin, and my best guess is it's come from the second drawer down, to the right of my kitchen sink, next to the butter knives. There is a stack of horror blades in there amongst the cockroaches and crumbs. It amazes me to think how many murder weapons we leave innocently lying around, often in perfect view of whatever crazed madman wanders in. Why would you ever bother to BYO? We may not be gun mad in this country, but the average Australian house is more kitted out than Abu Ghraib. There's golf clubs and hammers, spanners and knives, cricket bats, torches and rolling pins, not that I own half of those things, but I bet most of you do.

Miss Manga rushes into the house and straight to Chief, presenting it to him like he's the coach and she's about to renegotiate her salary package. I'm really milking this sporting metaphor, right? Suffice it to say, she's beaming and he looks impressed.

"Good work, Deana," he says, inspecting the knife, then handing it across to Thunder Thighs.

"Is that mud, do you think?" Deana asks, pointing to the mushy brown stuff smudged into the blood across the blade.

"Could be faeces," Thunder Thighs suggests, and Deanna recoils, as well she should.

I am equally shocked. What kind of animal stabs me in the back then defecates on the weapon before not quite chucking it into the nearest creek?

Just when we think the atmosphere can't get any more charged, another copper clomps down the stairs in plastic-covered booties and announces, "There's something you need to see in the kid's room, Chief."

My stomach does a backflip.

"Good? Bad? Ugly?" Chief asks, and he smirks.

"Tasty, I think."

Now I'm really confused.

While they head upstairs and vanish into Bob's room—which, yes, is *still* unavailable to me, thanks very much—I find myself distracted by a flashing light. It's not coming from the granny-beckoning tunnel although the annoying old biddy is still there, her mouth like a frozen yawn.

"In a minute, Gran!" I call out. "I need more time!"

Honestly, I don't remember her being so annoying in life.

Flash goes the light again. I glance into the kitchen where the woman in the green onesie is wielding an enormous digital camera and taking oddly angled photos of me. She's getting uncomfortably close.

I always loathed having my photo taken and didn't my mum know it. She'd whip out the old Nikon and try to corral Dad and I in front of whatever tourist trap we happened to be visiting, but inevitably the happy-snap was less happy and more snappy—Dad's teeth clenched into a stiff smile, me scowling fiercely, Mum wondering why she bothered.

I do thank God I'm not Gen Z though. They can't seem to get through breakfast without taking a selfie. It must be exhausting.

Snap! There goes the camera again, zooming in on the now-maroon bloody splotch between the red polka dots. These bright ghoulish images will no doubt be pored over later, first by Chief and his team, then by a pack of pasty lawyers and, eventually, by a jury of pissed-off peers who couldn't come up with a decent enough excuse to get out of jury duty and are now lumped with staring at my frumpy corpse.

How can anyone ever expect a fair trial when jurors don't sign up willingly? I mean, they have to be threatened with a fine, right? Well, here's a better idea. Why not invite interested parties to participate in court cases? Pop an invite in every mystery novel sold in local bookshops. Blast ads during *Law & Order*. Appeal to those who are naturally curious and love a complex puzzle, not the bored and useless.

I'm sorry, but if you're not smart enough or busy enough to get out of jury duty, I don't want you deciding my case, not if my son's life depends upon it. He'll be at the mercy of a bunch of dumb no-hopers who can't see their way out of a ziplock bag. Will it be one of those open-and-shut cases that are over in days? Or will they labour over the evidence for weeks, and will my son be standing in front of them, wrists in cuffs, his head on the block?

Not if I have anything to do with it.

I need to focus my energy. I stare hard into Bob's room. I want to see what all the fuss is about, but all I get is darkness, just a big black nothing where his bedroom should be.

It is still not open to me, and I cannot understand why. *What the hell is going on, Death? How fair is that?*

To add insult to injury, the photographer is now being called away from my corpse to photograph whatever tasty morsel has just been discovered in Bob's bedroom.

Gee, thanks a lot.

After another minute, Chief reappears on the landing, Thunder Thighs by his side.

"Let's get them both to the lab, hey, Tandia?" he says, nodding down towards a second plastic bag in Thunder Thighs' hands.

It looks like it contains a plate. One of my dinner plates, from the wedding set Cass's parents gave us, begrudgingly no doubt. They never liked me much, but let's not get distracted by that. They're both gone now, which is a pity because I'd love to plant it on one of them. Oh well, good riddance is all I can say.

What I want to know is, what is this Tandia person

doing with my good Wedgwood? And what did they just find in my son's bedroom that has them looking so pleased with themselves?

Why? I want to scream to Death or the Devil or whoever's in charge of this nightmare I've landed in. *Why let me see some things and not others? Why torture me this way? Are you demented?*

That's when I feel a light tap on my shoulder and swing around to find my grandmother standing just behind me, an expression of utter irritation on her wrinkly old face.

Oh dear, I think Gran has gone AWOL.

CHAPTER 13

I never really knew my grandmother. I mean, I thought I did, but I couldn't have. I was just sixteen when she carked it, and everyone knows how self-obsessed teenagers are. Most of us can't see past our own fringes and, in my case, it was a shaggy lump of hair that covered half my eyes.

I was a scrawny little thing with too much hair and a giant chip on one shoulder, mostly because I was an only child and it embarrassed the crap out of me. In an era when everybody had a baker's half dozen, I longed to be part of a large and boisterous family. I'd been to dinners at other girls' houses. I knew how these things went, the jostling for the best seat, the fighting over the last lamb chop. Dinner at my place was just, well, quiet.

It seemed to me that everyone else's families were so much fuller and more robust than mine. I don't know why my parents stopped at one, but I blamed that for my inability to get on with my peers. Other kids seemed so juvenile as a consequence. I couldn't relate to children and often wondered if I'd been saddled with a stack of bothersome brothers and sisters, things might have played out differently. If I'd been subjected to nightly taunting over the tuna casserole, I might have grown up more chilled out, more able to play the game. I certainly wouldn't have got tangled with Cass, also an only child and equally as wound up.

But you know, apart from that little glitch, my

childhood was relatively benign. I need to emphasise that. I didn't get neglected or abused or shoved off to boarding school (that'll make sense later). My parents were bleedingly, boringly normal. They loved me. I loved them back. That was that. I wish I could tell you they were crazed psychopaths, à la Sarah Burleigh. I wish I could somehow blame them for all this, but honestly folks, nothing to see there.

I was just a bit lonely, that's my only gripe.

Of course it didn't help that we lived far away from the only other family I had, the one who might have taunted me at the table and fought me for the last chop.

Grandma was a shadowy figure I never really figured out. She was so distant, and I don't just mean that metaphorically. Cornelia Gold, that's her real name, lived on the other side of Australia, which is a big deal. It's a big country. She rarely phoned and only visited every year or so, usually accompanied by a waft of lemony perfume and a bag of chewy mints, which she would deny me all day then offer just as I slipped into bed.

"I'm sending you the dental bill, Cornelia!" my mother screamed the first time she caught her. Gran only chuckled and offered them again the next night.

They never seemed to get along, my mum and Gran, and in retrospect I've got to wonder whether Gran only snuck me those treats to piss my mother off.

I can see now they had a very fractious relationship on account of the fact that my mother had dared to steal Cornelia's son away and move to the "back of Bourke." This place is actually only a few hours from Brisbane, but it might as well have been another planet. At least that was the story Mum stuck to, and Dad never contradicted it. He seemed quite chuffed by the idea of two women fighting over him.

What is it with men?

"Oh that's utter nonsense, your mother and I got on like a house on fire! Preferred her to my son if you really must know."

That's Gran again, standing to my right now in case you've been wondering.

She's holding something white and fluttery and still has a frown on her face.

"Look," I tell her. "I'm sorry you had to sneak out, but I'm not ready, okay? You can't just wrestle me into the tunnel."

She scoffs. "I'm not trying to wrestle you anywhere, you silly little girl. I've been trying to help you solve your murder. I have something for you that will explain everything."

Okay, that shut me up.

It turns out the old girl has been trying to advise me from the start and I have ignored her mad motioning, assuming she was only doing her duty as chaperone into the never-never.

"If you'd come to the tunnel in the first place, I could have given you this an hour ago," she hisses. "Instead, I had to go to a lot of trouble to get special permission to come out, and that's no small feat with my bung hip."

"I thought things like bung hips would be gone once we got to…" Is it heaven back there? I'm too scared to ask.

"It's called Forever," she says (is she reading my mind?), "and bodies are a complete waste of space there, but once we leave Forever, we revert back to our final life form which, in my case, is a wizened-up old hag." She stops and surveys her withered hands. "You know, I can't believe I ever got this old and wrinkly, but then I shouldn't complain, at least I made forty."

I gasp. Is my beloved grandmother really mocking my premature death?

"Oh suck it up, buttercup," she chides. Aha! She is reading my mind! I knew it! "One of my besties back there was killed in a car crash at just six. You've done all right."

"You hang out with a six-year-old?"

She stares at me. "That's what you took from my last sentence?"

"Just wondering."

She sighs. "There is no *age* in Forever. No bodies. We're just, well, spirits I think the living like to call it. Age and bodies are an earthly nuisance, but they have their benefits, like when dealing with you lot. It helps to look familiar to the ones we help across."

"Across?"

"To Forever!" She snaps her fingers. "Keep up please, Lulu darling, we haven't got much time! If I had come out as my best self—thirty-three if you must know, God I was a stunner back then, everything lovely and tight, and so much wiser than I realised—well you would never have recognised me, would you? You might have ignored me even more than you have done."

"I'm sorry Gran, but I won't rest until I know who killed me. I can't just skip off into the light as if nothing happened."

"I know that, you silly girl! That's why I'm here! You need to listen up. They'll be demanding my return any minute now, it's highly unorthodox."

"Well if you've come to tell me not to bother—"

"I've come to tell you how to get what you need before you enter the light."

She shoves a piece of paper towards me. At least it looks like paper, but it feels like an iPad screen and is as fluid as water.

"Read that. Carefully. It'll explain a few things and stop all your moaning. Now I've got to get back. If I stay out too long, my name will vanish from the register and I'll be doomed to spend eternity out here with all the other lost souls, watching the living fuck up time and again."

"Grandma!" I cry, and she chuckles.

"Just because I have to wear this old granny torso doesn't mean I have to sound like one!" Her face softens.

"Good luck, my darling, I know you'll do great."

As she glides back towards the light, I have a sudden panic attack.

Hanging around doesn't sound so idyllic anymore. I love my son, but turning into a "lost soul" isn't where I see myself in five years' time. I glance around furtively. I don't see any grumbling ghosts or rattling chains, but what if I also miss the register? What if I get locked out with the other spooks?

I hate ghosts. Always have. I never even read Casper comics when I was a kid. He was creepy and needy and had a really ugly fat, bald head.

"How long have I got?" I call after Gran who is just reaching into the tunnel.

She stops and looks back at me. "Long enough!" she calls back. "I hope!" she adds with an evil cackle.

And then she vanishes. Just like that. The light's still on, the tunnel still beckons, but the entrance is now empty. I am clearly on my own.

I glance down at the piece of paper she has given me. It's a set of rules authored by Death, and a scan of the first few quickly proves what I was beginning to suspect.

Death is a real stick-in-the-mud.

CHAPTER 14

The Rules of Death
©Forever

1. Thou shalt not hear what the living do not wish thee to hear

2. Thou shalt not see what the living do not wish thee to see

3. Thou shalt not invade the living's thoughts unless invited in

4. Thou shall see all when thou is open to seeing

5. Thou shall make thy way towards the light at the earliest opportunity

6. Once registered at Forever, thou shalt not return beyond the light without express permission

7. Thou shall be granted one final wish upon entering the light

Goodness, someone's got the hots for Shakespeare. It's all a little hoity-toity don't ya think? Perhaps they should add a few more LOLs and get with the twenty-first century.

In any case, that seventh rule has cheered me up enormously. Who knew Death was going to grant me a final wish, à la *I Dream of Jeannie*? I'm very excited by this and am already contemplating exactly what it is I'd wish for. I wonder if you're allowed to be a clever clogs and use your one wish to ask for endless wishes?

Or are they onto that?

Either way, there is so much I want; I barely know where to start. I want to live again! I want to give my son one more hug. I want to condemn NagHag and Cass to a life of utter misery! Oh and I wish Toadface's penis would drop off.

I could go on forever, but it's clear my drone's batteries won't last forever, so I need to concentrate. I'm rereading the rules, and I have to tell you I'm now feeling both annoyed and relieved. I mean, it's obvious Death is a stickler for privacy, and it certainly explains what I have seen and heard so far and what has been blotched out.

I wondered why I couldn't see the murderer sneaking away or why I couldn't watch my ex snoring through the doorbell. They clearly didn't *want* me to see. And Bob clearly doesn't want me anywhere near his bedroom—or the bathroom for that matter.

It's incredibly frustrating not to have access to everything, but I also know, deep down, it will probably be a relief later. Because, let's face it, my son is now thirteen, in case you'd forgotten that. Do I really want to spend the next few years watching him turn into a hormonal teenager under his bedsheets?

I think not.

Although I must say I am rather annoyed by Rule #4. What the hell is that about? I *am* ready to see! I am! What more can I do to prove this? Can I be any more murdered? Can I be any more dead? I've enlisted you, haven't I? I've hung around and watched things that nobody should have to watch, like people poking at my corpse and my beloved son sobbing into his sleeve.

Surely that rule is redundant?

Oh well, nothing I can do about it now. So let's try to work with what we've got and do as Gran suggested and stop moaning about the rest.

I can see most things, but not all. I can hear any conversations I choose to tune into, except the really private. And I can tell you right now, after the excitement of the first hour, there's not a lot of conversing going on.

Things appeared to have come to a grinding halt. It's as though everyone is on slow-mo or are having a smoko. In fact, that's exactly what a couple of cheeky coppers are doing down by the creek, dragging surreptitiously on ciggies while pretending to search the premises. Even Chief and Thunder Thighs, sorry Chasin and Tandia, look like they're gaggin' for a fag, perched on the edge of my staircase, arms dangling from their knees. They look pooped or perplexed or something.

I'm feeling a little shagged myself. Why don't we take a breather too? Why not make a theoretical cuppa, put our feet up, and assess where things are at?

Let's look at the clues first, if you don't mind, starting with the black shoes I saw as I toppled to the floor.

I'm no longer convinced they were Converse and not just because I'm trying to steer you away from my son. Well, maybe that's what it is. But I have to wonder now whether I associate all black shoes with Bob's favourite brand. I've never been one for fashion as I said. Let's try to keep an open mind about that, shall we?

So, black shoes. The culprit was donning them. We know that.

The second piece of evidence is just as compelling and equally as obscure—the bloody knife, which may or may not be covered in faeces. Ewww. Chasin has rushed the knife to the lab, along with one of my Wedgwood Cornucopias, so there's no point second-guessing until we know the facts.

Let's move past that for now. Let's consider the kitchen light that had been switched on. You noticed that one, right? I really hope you did. I've mentioned it twice now, and I can't be doing all the heavy lifting—really, I can't.

Here's the thing: I'm out of work at the moment, thanks to Toadface and his toady wife, so I am very careful about my budget and wasting money on things like electricity. I'm no NagHag, but I do regularly remind my son to flick the lights off as he leaves a room. It's not just a budget thing, it's his environmental duty, not that I'll be around to reap the rewards.

So why was it still on?

I know I wouldn't have forgotten to switch it off, I'm stingy that way, and I'm pretty sure I was the last person to leave the kitchen last night. Did Bob get up at some point after lights out? Was he wandering through the house aimlessly or, worse, with purpose?

I'm looking at the light now, and I'm frowning. I've always hated that light. It's an ugly amber-coloured 1970s retro tulip-shaped jobbie that came with the house. I'd always meant to replace it. And now I'm gone and it's still there and people will think, "Oh dear, what ugly taste she had in lights."

It's not like the house is any great chop, but it wasn't *ugly*. Small, sure, a little pokey, even a little dark, but it had a kind of charm, or at least I thought it did when we moved in when I was six months pregnant.

Cass and I bought this place together, just after we got married. It was smaller than we wanted, but it was all we could afford with the meagre savings that we had. The day we signed the papers was one of the happiest days of my life. I was full of anticipation back then, bursting with hope and optimism. I didn't see the sledgehammer that would soon come along and knock me flat again.

Later, after that sledgehammer had done its worst, I half expected Cass to fight me for the place, demand we sell it and split the proceeds. But he never did. I guess he figured his mistress had a bigger house that's more perkily renovated, so why bother? I bet she doesn't have any ugly orange lights.

Back to that. I honestly don't know if I left it on last night, but I'm not sure it has anything to do with anything. After all, the killer came in this morning, after sunup. I was murdered at precisely 9.25 a.m., in case you haven't been doing the maths. He wouldn't need to flick the light on.

Surely it's irrelevant?

Let's move on to something more pertinent, like the television set and the fact that it, too, was switched on. There is no way that was on when I came down this morning. You can see it clearly from the staircase, and I would have noticed if it was on. So it has to have something to do with whatever happened to me, right? That has to be evidence, of what I do not know.

It's still on, by the way. One copper and at least two forensic types are currently seated on my sofa watching *Days of Our Lives*. Seriously. They are catching up on a soap opera while a real-life, flesh-and-blood soap opera unfolds before their eyes. I can only assume theirs is more entertaining and wonder what I could have done to maintain their attention. Perhaps if I'd been stabbed by my ex-husband's father's illegitimate brother and was currently in a coma, my face fully made up, a sexy negligee on?

Still, we haven't yet explained what that TV was doing on. Did the killer flick it on to drown out the sound of my screaming (not that I ever got the chance)? It seems the only likely scenario. I didn't watch telly last night, was up in my room sulking if you must know, and I certainly didn't flick it on this morning. The last time I watched morning TV, I was breastfeeding Bob.

I doubt Bob turned it on either. Why would he? He never watches the box. He's Gen Z. They live for their iGadgets. TV is *so* last century. Not that Bob has many gadgets, I might add. He has a very "old" (read: "old" in computer years; it's still a spring chicken if you ask me) laptop on which he watches bad American crap about zombies or the apocalypse or both, and no "smartphone" to speak of—or into as the case may be.

I don't own one either. We may be the last two creatures alive sans a mobile phone, and I can't understand why parents happily hand their children these cancer-causing devices. Because mark my words, people, in thirty years' time, you'll all be joining class actions against Apple and Samsung. That is if you can find the energy between chemotherapy sessions. And you'll all be so shocked and outraged! You never knew! You never suspected! The fact that your ears began to boil after two minutes on your mobile was by the by.

Look, I'm no Luddite, right? I'm not against digital technology and portable phones and such. Really, I'm not. In fact, I quite like the idea of keeping in touch with my son. Perhaps if I had, he may never have snuck into that hutch with Henrietta and maybe I'd still be standing upright, making toast.

We can't know for sure, but what I do know, what I'm willing to put bets on, is that mobile phones give you brain cancer and that TV was switched on by a cold-blooded killer with a penchant for morning TV and/or a desire to hide his crime from the neighbours.

Speaking of which, the next piece of evidence is equally compelling—the presence of all those people at my doorstep on or around the time of my murder and the absence of the only one who should have been there. My ex-husband.

Perhaps it's time we took a closer look at Cass.

CHAPTER 15

Cassowary Jones was born to wealthy diplomats in Port Moresby, the shabby capital of Papua New Guinea, which helps explain his name. I mean, it doesn't quite excuse it, but they clearly had a deep love for their adopted country and its flightless fauna, either that or a very dark sense of humour.

So he grew up in a giant mansion behind razor wire with two security guards at the front gate and a watchdog he could never pat on account of the fact that it was part-Doberman, part-Rottweiler ("Rotterman" just doesn't do it justice). He tried to pat it once, and it nearly ripped his arm off. One of the aforementioned security guards had to clobber him over the head with his baton (the dog, not Cass), and while said dog forfeited Cass's arm after much persuasion, neither of them ever looked at each other the same way again.

How do you trust anyone when your own pet looks at you sideways?

It didn't help that his folks, being Australian diplomats, were constantly entertaining. Others, not him. There were cocktail parties, four-course dinner parties, tennis parties and parties that involved martinis and Mah-jongg, and he was shut out from the lot. And by shut out, I mean literally outdoors with a bottle of Fanta and a *Phantom* comic to keep him company. There was no TV up there back then and no friends within a five-kilometre radius.

He told me all this in the very early days when we still pretended we were a proper couple.

"I saw the world through smudged louvers," he said, showing a rare poetic flourish. "As soon as someone visited, I was ejected to the other side of the glass."

"But didn't you have a pool and a tennis court and shit like that outside?" I had asked, and he scowled.

"That's beside the point, Lulu. They're no use to me when there was no one to enjoy them with."

Still, I thought. Better than being stuck outside with a lump of coal.

"What about school friends?" I persisted.

"Didn't have any. The *hausgirl's* son came up occasionally, but that was that."

Yeah, yeah, bring out the violins, poor little rich boy and all that. Still, it does explain why he leaves the curtains open when he makes love, right? He thinks life is to be lived through transparent glass.

But here's the thing: being evicted outdoors was not the worst thing that ever happened to Cass, no siree. A greater injustice was to come. At the tender age of thirteen, he was shipped off to boarding school in Australia, and he blamed his mum.

I'm not quite sure why she should take the rap. I mean, it was his dad's fault they were even in PNG in the first place. His dad was the Australian high commissioner, not his mum, but it was his mum he blamed. Such is the plight of mums everywhere. He never forgave her for that final rejection. He could no longer watch the life he was supposed to lead through smudged louvers, he would now be barred from seeing anything. I guess he figured that was worse.

And so it was he attended a posh boys school in Brisbane where I gather the benign neglect ended and he was nagged within an inch of his life—by the schoolmasters, the brothers and the teachers. The only ones who didn't nag him were the other kids. They didn't even bother to bully him, he'd revealed. They just pretended, like his mother, that he didn't exist.

"Why? Why would they do that?" I had demanded.

"I don't know," he replied, defensively, and that was that.

Over the years, I have come to understand why. He is a bloody weirdo! He leaves his breastfeeding wife, he makes love in front of open windows, he has serious mummy issues.

Oh my God, there's our motive!

I knew we'd get to it if I just kept rambling long enough. Cass loathed his mother for sending him away. Did he hate me because I was about to do the same thing to his son? *And at the same tender age?* Was that why he stabbed me, because I was about to inflict a similar injustice upon thirteen-year-old Bob?

I'm shaking my head, metaphorically. I'm not enthralled with my own case. I mean, come on, I wasn't banishing my son to another continent. He was crossing the road to live with his other parent, one who did love him. I know that. For all his kookiness, Cass was a good dad.

Still, it makes you wonder: Where was my kooky ex when I was being slaughtered? Comatose from Stilnox, as he claims? Or was he fleeing my kitchen, bloody knife in hand, via the kitchen doorway (and a potential toilet stop)?

Oh, and there's a new piece of evidence we have to consider. While I've been waxing lyrical about my ex, the forensic team have got off their lazy arses and found something interesting beneath my cooling corpse.

It's long and blond, and it didn't come from my head.

CHAPTER 16

It may look like a simple strand of hair, but that follicle is the best news I've had all morning. We have another clue, and this one points away from my son, whose hair is a rip off of every second footballer in the European Champions League. It's dark brown and shaved short on one side with a little quiff at the top. I told you it was sharp.

Thank God Bob worships Cristiano Ronaldo and not Chris Hemsworth.

Chief isn't quite as excited as me when he is given the news, but he watches as the forensic team places the hair in yet another plastic bag, and then he stares at it for a few minutes before stepping outdoors and looking about.

He's clearly hunting for blondes. We should look too.

Okay, so who are our sandy suspects? It's a pity my ex-husband's hair is boring brown and Junnifer's is cherry red, but there's always Brenda isn't there? She has the most perfect blond hair of the lot. But isn't her alibi rock solid? Wasn't she coaching an entire soccer team while her perfect blond daughters were running around, no doubt scoring hat tricks? We should double-check that.

I also think of Psycho Sarah. Now, she's not blond, her hair's as black as her heart, but her daughter Henrietta is blond. Ish. Well, dirty blond, really, more drab brown than anything else, but that doesn't mean there wasn't one lighter strand in amongst the mix. Did that blond strand drop to the ground just before she stabbed me in the back?

Could Henny Penny have done this? Or her mum, who might have shed one of her daughter's hairs in the process?

Oh, hang on a minute.

I hate to be a killjoy, but it's just occurred to me that the blond hair could be a red herring. All we know at this stage is that the hair was present at the scene of the crime, but we don't know if it was dropped there by the killer—was it theirs or someone they'd recently hugged?—or by someone who'd visited my kitchen days earlier. It could be another annoying coincidence. It's not like I vacuum my kitchen floor every day—or every week for that matter—and I did have at least two blondes visit me in the past few days. And both of them are going to take a bit of explaining, starting with my stalker, Fiona Palaszczuk.

Fiona was an old high school mate. Okay "mate" may be stretching it. Friend of Last Resort would be more apt. We occasionally found ourselves sitting side by side at lunchtime or in class, two bored loners in a world full of BFFs. She didn't seem to know what to make of the other kids' boisterous immaturity either. We never really hung out, not unless we had to. Yet that ambivalence didn't stop Fiona from tracking me down through Facebook twenty years later and demanding my friendship. I guess she never found her BFF.

Would love to reconnect!! she wrote, exclamation marks all hers. *Hope you accept! I always had a minor crush on you!!! lol!!!*

WTF?

See, that's the bit where most of you would start madly tapping the Delete button on your keyboard, removing the friendship request. Some of you would even click "block" just to be safe, but not me. I seem to be a sucker for punishment, a magnet for mayhem. I thought, what the hell, I only have twenty-three friends (all complete strangers, apart from Bob who almost never participates), one more couldn't hurt.

Besides, according to Fiona's "About" box, she lived in Melbourne, a city far, far away. Which is why I nearly choked on my skinny cappuccino when I bumped into her at the local café about two months back.

"What are you doing here?" I asked.

"Visiting my sister, of course!" she replied, and it didn't exactly fill me with relief.

That's right, she was related to Psycho Sarah. I had forgotten that.

Being a polite person (and because she kept glancing down at the empty chair beside me), I suggested she join me for a coffee, and we had a nice enough chat. Then, after about an hour, she said good-bye, leaned down, placed her lips firmly on mine and kissed me smack on the mouth.

The kiss lasted less than a second, it was over before I had a chance to react, but I was flabbergasted. *What the hell was that?*

Now, don't get all PC on me. I have nothing against girls kissing. Hells bells, love who you want. Just don't love me when I don't love you back. And don't kiss me on the lips unless you're my lover. Got it?

That's when it finally occurred to me that the woman was unhinged. Still, I wasn't too perturbed. I would just go home, unfriend her, and that would be the end of it.

Oh how wrong I was.

Two weeks later, I ran into Fiona again. Or rather, she ran into me. On my own driveway.

I was just waving Bob off. He was heading to Bouncy Bounce with Sebastian. That's a place where, in case you haven't worked it out, you pay a ridiculous sum of money to watch your children smash into each other on a giant, inflated pillow. Apparently, it's called fun, but all I could see was endless weeks at the fracture clinic.

"I do not want him doing stupid tricks and breaking his leg," I told Junnifer, knowing she would probably be so busy checking her nails she wouldn't be watching.

"They'll be *fine*, Lulu darling! They're healthy lads!"

"Still made of flesh and bone, Jenny, so please keep a beady eye on Bob."

"We'll be back in two hours, and your son will be in one piece, I can assure you of that!"

He'd better be, I thought just as a vaguely familiar voice called out from behind us. "Hello there!"

Junnifer and I swung around to find Fiona standing at the edge of my lawn, leering up at us like a frisky postman.

My heart plunged. My eyes squinted. I thought, *Stalker alert!*

"What are you doing here, Fiona?" I never gave her my address. I made sure of that.

"Just wandering past," she said, "walking Sarah's dog."

Now I noticed the curly white mutt on a leash at her feet.

That's Psycho Sarah's dog? I thought she ate poodles for breakfast. Why is it that all the crazies have such tiny pets? A giant, slobbering Alsatian would have been more her style, or a Great White.

"Oh, really?" I said, not believing this ruse.

"Yeah! I moved into Sarah's granny flat. Did I tell you that?"

No, I thought coldly, you did not. A shiver ran through me. She was staring at Junnifer and the boys now, her leer turning lascivious, so I quickly did the introductions and got them safely on their way, then mumbled something about chores and scuttled inside.

Two hours later, Fiona was back, sans poodle, plus a bag of freshly baked muffins.

"Boys not back yet?" she said, glancing down the road.

I shook my head no. She giggled.

"I wanted to see if they came back with a sprained ankle!"

I'm so happy my son's bone health amuses you so much, I wanted to say, but instead, I did the silliest thing imaginable. I invited her inside for a cuppa! Talk about red flag to a bull. What was I thinking?

These tea visits became a regular occurrence after that. She'd casually drop in, baked goodies in tow, look around, sip tea and take off. But I never let her kiss me on the lips again, no way, José. All she got was a cold cheek and the brush-off.

Fiona's last visit was the day after film night. She brought her usual muffins, macadamia and white chocolate this time, and I gently steered her away from revealing what we both now understood: she wanted it badly and I didn't want to know. She stayed an hour, mostly staring at me looking constipated, like she had something to get out and didn't quite know how to say it. I knew she wanted to confess her undying love, and I wasn't having any of it, so I was relieved when Junnifer dropped Bob home and I could fob her off.

But here's the thing—the reason I've been waffling on—Fiona has blond hair! Of course hers comes straight from a bottle, that much is obvious, and it's a shaggy kind of bob à la Meg Ryan. It's not exactly long, but it's definitely blond. Did we notice how long the strand was? I can't recall.

Fiona may still be a suspect.

She could have dropped a strand of hair on one of her visits, or she could have dropped it this morning after stabbing me for refusing to return her advances.

Sound unlikely? Don't be disheartened, I have an even better suspect.

CHAPTER 17

The second visitor I had this week was NagHag, who, as we all know, is as blond as a slutty Swedish backpacker. Even though she lives just a bedroom window away, NagHag's visit had been a major surprise. I'm not sure she'd ever stepped inside my house before. Obviously she's come to the door plenty of times, to collect Bob or hand over his lunch box or "perfectly pressed uniforms" (her words, not mine, like I give a shit about that stuff), but never really *into* the house, into my kitchen where I felt compelled to offer her tea like this was a perfectly acceptable social visit.

She refused the tea, more's the pity. I really wanted to dazzle her with one of Fiona's muffins, pretend like I was the consummate "baking mom." I decided to offer her a muffin anyway, and she simply frowned and said, "Are they gluten-free?"

I could have shoved that muffin down her gob.

Anyway, this was no social call, NagHag quickly informed me. She was here to talk, mostly about Cassowary (she always used his full name and always with a straight face).

"I think Cassowary is seeing someone," she told me, like I was going to offer my condolences.

"Suck eggs, you blond wench! It's the least you deserve! May he have five children with the new one and leave you feeling as washed up as seaweed!" was what I *wanted* to say.

Instead, I swallowed my smile and said, "How do you know?" thinking, *So this is what karma feels like.*

She looked shamefaced. "He's been disappearing at odd hours of the day, sometimes for hours at a time. Comes home reeking of coffee."

"Coffee?"

"Exactly!"

She said it as though she could now rest her case.

I looked at her sideways. Surely smelling of perfume or booze or, heaven forbid, *sex*, was more incriminating, but then she said, almost nonchalantly, "That's how he fell in love with me, of course."

Whoa! I did not need to know what they supped between lovemaking sessions thank you very much.

Her icy-blue eyes squinted. "So you don't know anything? He hasn't mentioned… someone else?"

"I'm pretty sure I'm the last one he'd tell."

"Really? It's just, well, he's been spending a lot of time over here lately, hasn't he?"

Now that she mentioned it, yes he has.

I didn't let Cass in the front door for the first few years. Whenever it was his turn to take Bob, I'd pack the little cherub up with his favourite teddy and a change of clothes, then dangle him like bait on the grass out front. Cass would scurry over and thank me profusely, rushing the poor kid across the road like I was going to suddenly change my mind and yank him back.

It did occur to me once or twice. I'm sure it occurs to all wronged parents, whether they'll admit it or not. I mean, revenge doesn't come much sweeter than denying your partner his kids, right? But it was Bob I didn't want to deny. I knew he needed a dad, even a deadbeat one like Cass, and so I swallowed my bitter little pill and handed him over, every second weekend until he was five. The custody arrangement loosened up after that, but I'd always insisted on having Bob home by Saturday night. I wanted Sunday mornings with my son.

And look where that got me—on a kitchen floor, with a hole in the back.

Anyway, I'm digressing. The point is, as the years went by, my anger towards Cass dissipated and lately we'd been holding civil conversations that lasted longer than five minutes at the front door.

A few months ago, I even waved him inside, only because I was on the phone and he was standing out there looking like a lost gnome. I offered him tea, he asked for coffee, and that was that. We talked for a good hour, and I'd forgotten what fun he could be, how he made me laugh. Now I've got to wonder if he was trying to tell me something, if there was something on his mind.

"It's only natural he'd come over, Brenda," I told her. "We do share a child."

She nodded. "Of course, sorry, I know he'd never go back to you. I know that."

That's when my blood began to bubble. "Having *said* that, we have become very *close*, lately. *Very* close indeed."

I let that sink in, then plastered a smile to my lips. "Perhaps I can talk to him for you? Next time he drops in. Help you sort this mess out?"

She shook her head wildly, her stupid blond pigtails flying about like a wind turbine. "No, no, I'm sure that's not necessary. I'm sure I can ask him myself."

Then something shifted in her, a kind of sadness entered her eyes, and she looked for a moment like she felt sorry for me. *Me?* I wasn't the one currently being cheated on!

"I'm glad you two are close again, Lulu," she said softly. "I do mean that. It has to be good for Bob to see his parents getting along. I know you were barely talking to each other at the end there."

"Sorry?"

"You know, when we… when he… I know you two hadn't been getting on for years."

Hadn't been getting on? I'd just had his bloody baby!

"I know that's why he reached out to me," she continued, completely unaware of my confusion—or perhaps fuelled by it. "Why he came over so often for cups of coffee and long chats. He was lonely. He needed to talk. One thing led to another."

My blood was boiling over now, and she must have finally noticed, or perhaps I'm being too kind. Perhaps she had achieved exactly what she'd hoped to achieve because she turned the heat down suddenly. "Anyhoo, that's water under the bridge, isn't it? I'd better get back; dinner must be ready by now. I'm making Bob's favourite, lasagne!"

Actually it's spaghetti bolognaise, but I wasn't about to give her the head's up, so I just watched as NagHag took off, a faux smile back on her face, and I couldn't help feeling a little like I'd been hit by a Mack truck.

I always remembered my marriage breakdown as a fast, furious process. He saw a sexy slut. He slept with her. He was out.

Did it really begin over something as benign as a cup of Mount Hagen Instant?

My mind suddenly wafts back to another time, another era, when things were so simple. When life was so innocent.

I am being swept back to my bedroom, to a night when Bob is just young. He is at my breast, and I am smiling. I cannot see Cass, but I can hear him. I can feel him. It is odd.

He is asking, "Can we... you know? Tonight?"

I can see myself on the bed. I do not answer, clearly mesmerised by my son.

"Please, Lulu," Cass says. "It's been a long time. I... I need this... I need you."

Finally I look up, a frown just edging out my smile. "Honey, I'm in the middle of feeding Bob."

"I know that," he says. "But after, when he's asleep, can we...? Maybe?"

My frown deepens, I turn my back to him and smile down at my child, but something is wrong with this image.

Bob is no longer a baby. Bob is a boy.

The next minute I am being rushed to the house next door, and this time I am looking at Brenda, who is holding her front door open, a strange look on her face. She is younger, she is brighter, and she is feeling sorry for me.

"Come on in," she says. "I'll pop the kettle on."

CHAPTER 18

Okay, what the hell was *that?*

I shake the thought away. My memory is getting twisted in knots. I'm seeing things that didn't quite happen, feeling things that make absolutely no sense.

I think we're losing focus.

The point is, there are a couple of blonde suspects we need to keep an eye on. For now, let's get back to the scene of the crime where things are moving forward again and my body is being gently lifted into a black body bag. It's lovely that they're being gentle, really it is, but I've got to wonder why they bother. It's not like I would know the difference.

While they're zipping the bag up, a commotion is starting up outside. The National Nine News team have arrived in their shiny white van looking all perky and important.

Well, what d'ya know, I'm gonna make the midday bulletin.

A woman with a starched blouse and matching hair jumps out from the front passenger seat and strides across the road towards my house. It looks for just a moment as though she is going to walk straight through the police tape, but no, it continues to work like a force field, and she stops short, indicating with a flurry of manicured fingernails to her camera crew to hurry the hell up. A tubby guy with rolling eyes and an afro is pulling a camera onto his shoulder, another bloke is fiddling with what looks like a microphone. As they slowly make their way over, another van screeches to a halt. This time it's the Channel Seven news crew and Starchy Chick has gone berserk, her nails in perpetual motion as she orders her crew with one hand and a nearby ogling officer with the other. She looks like she's directing aircraft. Give her a set of Ping-Pong paddles, and she'd have it down pat. It has little to do with me, of course. She just wants the scoop.

"Detective! Detective!" Starchy Chick cries out to the acne-faced officer who is clearly not a detective.

The officer looks slightly more invigorated now—the press! the press!—and strides across the yard towards her, careful to stay on her side of the police tape.

"How can I help you, madame?" she asks like she has no idea why the press would want a chat.

"Can I get a statement, please?" the reporter asks. "Can you tell us exactly what's happened here this morning?"

The officer glances around, then says, "I'll see if I can get my boss. Wait here."

And the frantic reporter does, but she's now joined by the Channel Seven guy in a shiny grey suit who's smiling cheerfully and with good reason. He didn't miss the scoop.

"Morning, *Mirelle*," he purrs, and she shoots him a dagger look.

"Get in the queue, Longbottom. I got here first."

"What queue?" He makes a show of looking around. "You haven't even got a vox pop lined up yet."

Chief appears then, a stony look in his eyes. He's not as starstruck as his officer, and I can already tell he won't be much use to those two who are wielding microphones and screaming questions at him like, "Detective Chasin! Can you tell us what happened? Can you give us a comment please?"

He simply steps under the police tape and says, "Later folks."

I catch a sly smile on his lips as he pushes past them

and towards Cass's place.

I want to smile smugly too, but the truth is I was keen to hear what he had to say. I want to hear his thoughts, find out whether he has any leads, a suspect in his sights.

Oh well, no news is good news I guess.

As the reporters start nagging their camera crew—something about "vox pops" and "fresh blood" and "hurry the fuck up!"—I see Junnifer beaming back at them. It's all she can do to keep from waving them over for a comment. And I think that's exactly what she's about to do when I notice Sarah walking towards her, arms on her hips.

She does not look friendly. But that's par for the course.

"What are you doing here?" Sarah says. Her voice is as steady as a sniper's rifle.

Still, it's a bloody good question, and one that hasn't been sufficiently answered yet.

Perhaps it's time to take a closer look at Junnifer, if only because I really can't stand the woman. That and the fact she was the first civilian on the scene, thus making it entirely plausible she was around when that blade dug deep into my back. I can't think why she would have it in for me. Do you kill someone because they call you Jenny? I doubt it, yet she was in the general vicinity at the time I was murdered.

Why, oh why?

I don't buy her, "I was just driving past" crap. There's as much chance of that as her hitching a ride to the greyhound track. Junnifer lives in a completely different part of town, the posher part in case you hadn't worked it out (and I hope you have because, really, I need you to be smart).

The truth is, I never really knew Junnifer. Apart from kid swaps, we never hung out together, rarely had a conversation that lasted more than five minutes. I always assumed she came from money—and with good reason.

Her house and car are fancy schmancy. Her accent, definitely private school, and the way she carries herself, the confidence… well, you don't get that in a demountable classroom on the wrong side of the tracks. I'm not sure if she's ever been married, there must have been someone once—à la Sebastian (his name another example of her poshness, am I right?).

In any case, there was definitely *no* play date organised with my son this weekend. I had cancelled all outings on account of that sleazy smooch in that rotting hutch. But there wouldn't have been a play date today anyway. There never was on a Sunday. As I said before, that was always my day with Bob whether he liked it or not. And increasingly the answer was *not*. Apparently, Sundays were the best days to hang with your mates, the day that friends had parties and played soccer and all that inane nonsense. Like they were more important than his mum.

No siree, this was *my* day, and Junnifer knew well enough to leave us alone.

So there's no good reason why Posh Pants should be driving past my house today, let alone soon after my murder, especially *without* her son.

Speaking of Sebastian, I'm not sure what she said to him, but he's still hanging about, now with a mayhem of mates beside him, each holding an iGadget, several clinging on to bicycles or skateboards, including Henrietta. I also see the do-gooder, ciggie-dobber from the bus stop, just behind them. Fran doesn't have any of those contraptions, but she does have tears in her eyes. She looks genuinely sad. Oh, that's so sweet! At least she's not torn between ogling the crime scene, tweeting one-liners and hitting the skate park.

But back to Junnifer. What's her motive I hear you ask? Good question. I know she likes my son, he's always been a great entertainer of hers, but removing me isn't going to hand him to her on a platter. He'll go to his dad.

Hang on a minute, perhaps we should listen in. Sarah is

getting quite worked up, her lumpy hands gesticulating wildly. It can't be too private because a few words flutter towards me on the breeze. Words like, "Can't bloody believe it!" and "Bloody well stop!"

Now Junnifer blushes. Oh, this looks intriguing.

"You think I didn't see you sneaking about here in the early hours this morning?" Sarah says, her voice as gruff as a quarterback. "I know you're up to something."

Oooh, do go on.

"Look, Sarah," Junnifer says, her voice audibly shaky, "I don't see what it's got to do with—"

"You think I'm going to look the other way? That I'm going to let you get away with your disgusting behaviour in my neighbourhood?"

What disgusting behaviour? What's she talking about, and does it involve a knife and my back? And if it does, how does Sarah know and why isn't she talking to the cops? I know she likes to fight her own battles, hell she starts most of them, but come on, woman, speak up!

Their conversation comes to a sudden halt as my front door swings open and a trolley is wheeled out. It's my body, of course, concealed within that suffocating body bag. No one can actually *see* anything—there could be an old surfboard in there for all they know—but it manages to enthral the crowd like a horror flick, and they watch, riveted, secretly delighted, as the forensic team start pushing me towards their van.

The news crews rush up excitedly, their vox pops ditched like little more than extras now that the leading lady has arrived. I know that's me. I know I'm their *raison d'être*, but it gives me no joy, no solace. I was never one of those pitiful creatures who craved fifteen minutes of fame. Could never even watch reality TV. I just didn't get why you'd deliberately flaunt your laundry in public. Or maybe it was just because my laundry was so damn drab (do I need to remind you of those Bonds undies again?).

Anyway, as the cameras zoom in, the forensics guys

carefully hoist me into the back of their van and then slowly drive away, no sirens blaring. There is no urgency.

I guess I'm off to a morgue somewhere and then onto the chopping block. I feel a little like the poor rat I had to dissect back in Year Seven and feel shame now that I took such delight. Will the coroner enjoy my dissection? I suppose that's not a bad thing. It's better to like your job, I realise, than recoil at the thought. Besides, maybe he/she will find more clues that will crack the case wide open, although I won't be around to witness it.

I know how those things work. Unlike your average one-hour crime show, autopsies aren't performed in the first ten minutes. They can take days, I believe, and it doesn't help that I live regionally. I will have to wend my way to a bigger city where I will be shoved into a cold box and onto a waiting list behind ten other corpses, a few guest lectures at the nearest university, and afternoon games of golf. By the time the coroner finally studies my cadaver for clues, I'll be long gone and you will have moved on to the new Patricia Cornwall novel.

That's why I have to bid my body farewell and stay put. The crowd might be fixated on my corpse, but it's as good as useless to us. We need to work with what we've got, and take a closer look at the crime scene, starting with the place where it all went belly up.

CHAPTER 19

The kitchen is now eerily empty. Everyone has cleared out. Even the burnt toast has been carted away as evidence of nobody knows what. All that remains is the bloody patch of linoleum. Who cleans that up, I wonder? I hope they're not leaving it for poor Bob. If so, they'll be waiting awhile. I could never get the lad to tidy his bedroom, let alone wash the kitchen floor.

That's when I remember. Of course! How could I forget? He *did* wash the kitchen floor, or at least he wiped up the milk he spilt there soon after trying to steal the birthday cake after dinner last night. Bob had the entire cake on a plate in one hand, glass of milk in the other, and was just making his escape when I strolled in.

"Arrgh!" he cried as though caught with a smoking joint, splashing half the milk across his shirt and the other half on the kitchen floor.

I raised my eyebrows. I stared pointedly at the milk and cake. He blushed profusely, then dumped both items on the bench and retrieved a wet sponge, which he used to start mopping up the mess. And by "mopping up," I mean spreading the mess farther.

I found a dry sponge under the sink and helped him get it under control although it took us a while. Why they say not to cry over spilt milk is beyond me, it's a bugger of a thing, all sticky and turning sour fast. Then, most of the floor glistening wet, he skulked out but not before I took the cake and placed it back in the fridge where it belonged.

Bob was not welcome to his birthday cake until he had the decency to speak to me. And not a nibble sooner. As I did all this, he gave me a look I had never seen before. It was as dark as the fudge icing on his fingers. He was angry. Really angry. And I remember being surprised by this. It's just cake, kiddo, and probably not a very good one if my previous efforts are anything to go by.

Still, that dark look haunted me long after he'd left the kitchen (haunts me again now if truth be told), which is why I'm so thrilled about the blond hair. See, that's the thing I want you to focus on, folks. Surely if anyone had dumped a blond hair here *earlier* than my murder, we would have wiped it up last night! We did a pretty thorough job; I am a cleaner after all. Or *was*, before Toadface tossed me out.

I think we can safely assume that whoever killed me, dropped their hair while doing it. Sort of like a memento. That blond hair has to belong to the murderer, right? Oh I hope so, because it eliminates my Bob. Don't forget, his hair is short and brown. Really, it's very short, and very, very brown.

Now, back to the cake. Are you thinking what I'm thinking? Should we check inside the fridge? I'm about to do just that when I hear a voice so familiar, so achingly beautiful, it's like a choir of angels singing another Leonard Cohen song.

"Mum? Ohhhhhh Mum."

Huh?

"Mum, can you hear me? Muuuuum?"

My heart has leapt in all its bloody gory into my throat. I think my son is calling out to me. Shhh! Let's shut up for a moment and listen.

"Mum, I'm so sorry, so, so, soooooooo sorry."

I feel a crush of despair. Yes, that is my son's voice, but he's not talking aloud, he's talking to himself, and he wants me to hear. Worse, I think he wants to confess. I feel sick, I want to scream, but then he says something that shuts me up.

"Oh Mum, I should never have let Seb give me that ciggie, and I should never have kissed Henny. I only did it to scare her off, but it didn't, and I never meant to—"

He stops. There is silence.

Why is there silence? What's going on?

I zoom back out of the kitchen and towards Cass's house where I notice Chief is now ringing the doorbell again. Damn you meddling cop!

The bell must have interrupted Bob's thoughts because within seconds he is opening the door, standing there, mute again.

What was Bob trying to tell me before Chasin interrupted? Why was he kissing Henny to scare her off? Didn't he know that would only *encourage* her? There's a reason it's called first base!

And what was he about to say? What did he *not* mean to do?

What?

I want to grab Bob by both shoulders and give him a shake, but Chief already has his grimy hands on one of them and is distracting Bob from his thoughts.

"How're you holding up, son?"

Bob shrugs. "All right I guess."

"That's the way. Could you do me a favour and fetch your dad, please?"

Bob withdraws, and now, finally, I can see into their house. It is no longer closed to me. Bob must be welcoming me in whether he realises it or not. I wonder what Cass and NagHag would have to say about that.

CHAPTER 20

Cass appears from a doorway to the right, shuffling down the long wooden hall. He has pulled on a collared shirt and appears to have brushed his hair, which is "short back and sides" in keeping with his bank Johnny job. I wonder if he is heading out or just wants to look good for the coppers. Or perhaps it's the media he's dressing up for because I can see a third van pull up outside, this one for radio station KZZ-FM. I think they need to reassess their motto "First with the local news!" Not today, bucko. Not by a long shot.

Chief has asked Cass if he can question him now, and Cass seems a little startled by this, which is quite silly of him. What did he think was going to happen? Did he honestly expect they would leave him alone to mourn the suspicious death of his ex-wife? The one he lives across the road from, within easy stabbing distance of?

They are both moving back inside, deep within the house, away from the media no doubt, but we can follow them in and I am thrilled by this, and not just because I can check out NagHag's rather gaudy interior design (all golds and creams and let's-pretend-we-don't-have-a-muddy-son whites).

Okay, that may not be important, right now let's focus on what the snivelling lowlife has to say for himself. Let's see what kind of performance he puts on for the police.

I almost feel like I'm watching a really bad

pantomime…

Scene 1: In the living room—midmorning
(Cass and Chief enter stage right)

Chief: "So you say you've been fast asleep since (pauses)… what time, exactly?"

Cass: (flustered) "Um, well, Brenny and the girls took off for soccer around…" (pauses) "Hun!" (silence) "Honey, you there?"

NagHag: (enters stage left) "Yes, sweetie?"

Cass: "What time did you clear out this morning with the girls?"

NagHag: "It was exactly 7.45 a.m. Had to be at the game by eight."

(Cass turns back to Chief as if that answers that, but Chief seems too interested in Brenda and not for all the right reasons. He is admiring her long legs, which are now naked, well, if you don't count the tiny denim shorts and killer wedges. Cass coughs, and Chief gives himself a shake.)

Damn you, Chief! I thought you were on my side!

Chief: "So what did you do after your wife and daughters left the premises?"

Cass: "Went back to sleep, of course."

Chief: "And you did not wake up again until…"

Cass: "Brenny came running in and woke me. I had taken a—"

Chief: (interrupts) "Sleeping tablet, yes, so you said." (pause for eye roll)

Okay, I made that bit up, but I bet he was eye rolling on the inside.

Chief: "So let me get this straight. You never saw your son this morning? Not until your wife woke you?"

Cass: "No, I said that. Lulu had Bob last night. She has him every Saturday night because she wants to wake him on Sunday. It's their little *ritual.*"

I don't like the way he said that word. Not one little bit. His tone sounds embittered. Did he begrudge me that?

Chief: "So there's nowhere else your son would have been?"

Cass: "What? No, of course not."

Chief: "And there was a birthday party yesterday, is that correct?"

Cass: "Well, there was a birthday. Bob turned thirteen, but there was no party. Lulu saw to that."

Enough with the bitterness already! I was teaching him a lesson. It's called moral fortitude, and you could do with some!

Chief: (refers to his notes) "Okay, so back to this morning. Let me see if I have this correct. There is no one who can vouch for your presence here, in bed, between 7.45 a.m. (checks notes again) and approximately 10.25 a.m. when your wife woke you? You were all alone?"

Cass: (flushes slightly) "I don't like what you're suggesting."

I can't say I blame him.

Chief: (frowning) "What exactly am I suggesting, sir?"

Cass: "You think I was with someone else at that hour, well you've got it all wrong. I wouldn't sleep around on Brenda!"

Huh?

(Chief and NagHag share a frown.)

NagHag: (clears throat) "Er, Cassowary, I think what Detective Chasin was actually suggesting was that because you were fast asleep, *alone*, you have no alibi for your ex-wife's murder."

(pause so audience can gasp)

I have to take a moment to gasp as well. It sounds to me like Cass is happier to be accused of murder than adultery. Well, that's gotta make you think, right?

Chief has ploughed on with another question, but Brenda's eyes have narrowed and she clearly is having a think because I can now hear her say, "Oh dear Lulu, you were right. The bastard *is* screwing around."

I'm not sure I ever actually said that and quite so colourfully, but if it makes her feel better… The point here is Brenda, too, has not spoken aloud. Her lips have not budged. They are wedged into a perfectly polite smile, but I know she is talking to me and she is not happy.

I wonder what Cass would say, knowing his wife is chatting subconsciously with his dead ex?

Cass is answering Chief now: "I last saw Lulu, I guess, yesterday. I stopped in for a cuppa at about…"

Yeah, yeah I know this bit. Cass stopped in, we chatted, yada yada. I'm more interested in Brenda's thoughts. She's working her way through a list of names, most of which I don't recognise.

"Teresa Hollows? Nah, too old for the lying bastard. Connie Chambers? Hmmm, not quite pretty enough. Leslie Movary? She'd probably be up for it…"

Ah, hang on a minute, Brenda, I have a better name for you, and you're not going to like it one little bit. She's young(ish), she's pretty, and I bet she's gagging for it.

How about Jennifer Cloak?

CHAPTER 21

Sebastian's mum must be sleeping with my ex!

Seriously, think about it. Junnifer was present at the time of my death, *sans* her annoying son. Cass was home in bed, *supposedly* alone. Well, I don't think so, folks.

I think Junnifer was having her merry way with my ex-husband while I was being slaughtered in a room across the street.

What a bitch.

She's not just deceiving Brenda and me, she's abusing her son's friendship, using both boys so she can get her manicured claws on Cass. And don't get me started on that philandering bastard; once a cheater always a cheater, but that's no excuse.

No wonder Junnifer was so defensive when the first officer asked if she knew where Cass was this morning. It also explains what Sarah was spitting about on the street just now.

"You think I didn't see you sneak about in the early hours this morning? I know you're up to something!"

Sarah wasn't accusing her of murder. She had busted Junnifer sneaking out of Cass's house! There's no other explanation; it just adds up.

Here's how I think it went down.

They must have started their traitorous tryst some time ago, which explains why Brenda was growing suspicious and why Cass started hanging at my place. He wasn't there to chat with me, he was hoping to run into his lover.

They obviously rendezvoused in Cass's bedroom this morning, right after Brenda and the girls left for soccer. Then, hearing all the commotion outside, Cass must have sent Junnifer out to retrieve his son while he pretended to be zonked out on Stilnox, to deflect attention.

Hang on a minute, that doesn't make a huge amount of sense. Why not sneak Junnifer out the back door and come fetch his son himself? Have I got that bit wrong?

Okay, so I haven't dotted all my i's yet, but this is getting very, very interesting. And I think Chief Chasin agrees because he's now watching Brenda who is watching Cass like a hawk. Her eyes are squinted tightly, and she's no longer talking to me, but I know exactly what she's thinking.

Chasin clearly does too because he says, "If I might have a word alone with your husband, please, Mrs Jones?"

For a second there I think she's going to throw herself on top of Cass and gouge his eyes out, but she doesn't. She just flashes him a "this ain't over, bucko!" look and walks out, while I have a little chuckle and settle in to watch.

If only we had some popcorn!

Chief waits until he can no longer hear her clickety clack down the hallway, then asks, "Can you tell me a little bit about your ex-wife?"

Hang on a minute. Doesn't he want to question Cass about his affair? Get the goss?

"Like what?" Cass says.

"I'd just like to get a grasp on who Ms Gold was, maybe get an idea of why this happened. Do you know if she had any enemies, for instance?"

Cass smirks. "Ah, yeah, I'd say she had a few."

Really?

Chief says, "Like who?"

Cass pushes back into his seat. He seems uncomfortable. Good! He blows some air out of his lips.

"Look, Lulu had an annoying habit of rubbing people up the wrong way. She didn't make friends easily."

Okay, I might not be enjoying this as much as I thought I would.

Cass continues, "But I'm not sure that made anyone want to kill her."

"Did you know she had an AVO out against her?"

Now why'd he have to go and mention that?

Cass seems genuinely surprised to hear this. "Really? Who?"

Chief does not answer.

"Wow, well, I'm shocked. I mean, sure she could be harsh, cruel, even. Could cut people down with a word, a simple look. But I never saw her as threatening. Unless of course you tried to get between her and Bob. Then you had to watch your back."

He winces at his words—as well he should.

"Did you try to get between her and Bob?" Chief asks and I know what he's insinuating, but Cass doesn't seem to catch it. Did I mention he's not real bright?

"Nah. I lost that battle a long time ago."

"It was a battle? Was there a custody dispute?"

He snorts. "God no. I wouldn't've dared." He sits forward, places his palms together, prayerlike in front of him. "Look, I fell for Lulu the second I saw her, sitting, reading a book all by herself at that dingy Irish pub. It was love at first sight."

It was?

"I watched her for about an hour. She was like a tiny little bird, perched at the bar, sipping her glass of Chardonnay, but even then she looked like she needed nobody, like she couldn't care less about anything. I thought that was a good thing. I admired that about her."

"Er, Mr Jones," interrupts Chasin, "I'm not sure this is relevant."

No, no, let the man speak.

Cass rushes on. "The thing is, I got that wrong, see?

Lulu did need someone… She needed Bob. It's the reason we got married. I'm under no illusion she wanted me for me." He chuckles drily. "She wanted me for Bob. It's only later that I realised she wasn't sitting at the bar innocently reading a book, she was baiting a bloke, a sperm donor to father her child."

Oh come on! Now he's just being melodramatic.

Chief is suddenly listening to all this garbage as though it is somehow consequential, like it somehow has a bearing on this case, and it infuriates me.

What has my desire for children—a desire all women have, surely?—got to do with some bastard stabbing me in cold blood?

"Lulu was one hundred percent devoted to that kid," Cass continues. "No, make that *two hundred* percent. It wasn't healthy. It was like she had created a cult of two. She worshipped him and he worshipped her, and no one else was welcome. You know her full name's Ludovica, right?"

So? What's that got to do with anything?

"She was named after some mad king who built some stupid castle. That's the thing! She built a castle, or she tried to, all the way around her and Bob. A big, fortified castle that no one else could conquer."

My goodness, there's his poetic flair rearing its ugly head again.

Chasin asks, "Is that why you guys broke up?"

"In a nutshell, yeah. It's also the reason I stayed here, right next door. I know what everyone thinks. I know they think I'm flaunting my marriage at my ex-wife, that I'm some kind of arsehole. But that's not what it was about at all. God knows Brenda wanted to move, begged me many times over, but I couldn't do it." He glances around at his blinding-white living room, as though not quite sure how he ended up there. "I knew this was the only way I would see Bob regularly."

Chief doesn't say anything, so Cass continues. "Don't you see, it was all about protecting Bob. I could see how she was suffocating him, squeezing the bloody life out of the poor kid. That's why she wouldn't let him have an iPhone. It's the first thing cult leaders do, they isolate. They put up the drawbridge."

Oh now he's just mixing his metaphors!

"I was so happy when she told me she wanted Bob to live here now that he's thirteen. I thought maybe she had finally seen the light—"

"She said that?"

"Yes, check with Bob, she was throwing him out. Except, I knew it wouldn't happen or if it did it wouldn't last. She lived for that kid. There was no one else."

"We have evidence of at least one affair."

"Really?" He looks stunned again. "Well, that wouldn't have been serious. All she ever wanted was Bob, and it was killing him."

"Did that make you want to kill her?"

The sudden accusation takes him by surprise. Cass sits up straight.

"What?"

"Did you take matters into your own hands so you could free Bob from his suffocating mother?"

"No! Never! I didn't kill Lulu. I would never…"

Chief looks pretty pleased with himself. He wasn't trying to unpack me so much as stitch my ex-husband up, and I'm not sure whether to be relieved or sad. It's great they're pointing the spotlight away from my boy, and I'm not exactly feeling any loyalty to Cass right now. How dare he suggest I'm some kind of crazed sperm-gathering cult leader squeezing the lifeblood out of her son? It's called motherly love, and I make no apologies for it!

Yet I'm not entirely comfortable with the idea that the ex did it either. For starters, that means poor Bob becomes an instant orphan—his mother murdered, his dad locked up for life—and then there's the small matter of me still having a teeny weeny crush on the sick bastard.

Oh damn, did I say that aloud?

Yep, call it stupidity, loneliness, insanity, whatever, especially in the light of what we've just heard, but for the past few months I had been thinking what Brenda was thinking. I had been wondering why he was dropping over so much, whether he was starting to get interested in me again. Hell, I might as well admit, I had even considered keeping my doors unlocked at night. You know, just in case he snuck back in, but I didn't last night, you need to know that.

I locked that back door!

Chief suddenly switches direction and asks, "What about Bob?"

Cass says, "What about him?"

"You said he was being suffocated. Do you think he might have tried to free himself? Might have attacked his mum?"

"No! Never!" Cass cries, and now suddenly it's Chief I want to scream obscenities at. "He loved his mum."

Damn straight he did.

"He would never do anything to hurt her, never! God, he couldn't even tell her how much she was smothering him, didn't want to hurt her feelings. Sure, she sent him mad at times—he'd come over here ranting, crying. Sometimes it would take us hours to calm him down. She drove him nuts."

Oh shut up, Cass! Just shut up! All you're doing is corroborating Chasin's theory and being mean in the process. I really don't want to hear this rubbish, and I can't believe I can. I know how the rules work, this wouldn't be audible to me if Cass didn't want me to hear. He's obviously trying to hurt me, even now.

Jesus, Cass, is my death not enough? The castle's been demolished. Bob's free as a bird. Why besmirch my memory? Why make me sit through it?

Please, dear reader, don't believe everything I hear. Please don't take the word of a cheating bastard over mine.

I loved my son. Just enough. I didn't lock him away or squeeze the life out of him. I just loved him, that's all there is to it.

Although not for Cass, he's not finished with me yet.

He says, "You know she wanted to homeschool Bob until I talked her out of it."

Hey, it wasn't such a dreadful idea; the local school is hardly Trinity Grammar. Besides, I'm the one who has to sit through endless parent-teacher meetings being told how he "could do better" and "talks too much in class". He must get that from his step-mum.

"But I know Lulu loved Bob," Cass continues, "and he loved her back, and there's no way he did anything to hurt her, and nor would I. She wasn't perfect, my God far from it"—yes, yes, we get your point!—"but I loved her too, you know. So much more than she realised."

Well, that last bit came out of left field. But it's *too little too late, Mister!* You've just slandered me to the top detective and handed your son to him on a platter. You might as well fetch the handcuffs and read Bob his rights while you're at it.

Now the Chief must be thinking, *That woman sounds nuts, I'd stab her in the back, too, if she were my mum.*

Except he obviously doesn't want to act on it, at least not yet. Instead, he stands up and stretches like they were just chewing the fat.

"Right, well, I better get back to it. Please be sure to hang around, hey? In case I have more questions for you."

Cass nods and then drops back into his seat, his eyes closed tight. And I float above him feeling like I have been stabbed in the back all over again.

CHAPTER 22

As Chasin heads back to the crime scene, I am tempted to linger, see if Brenda appears with a set of knuckle-dusters and a baton. I can't clobber the guy, but if she could do the honours, that'd be great.

No such luck.

Brenda is perched on the edge of a king-size bed in the master bedroom, I guess. It's all floral wallpaper and lavender candles, like a scene from *The Bold And The Beautiful*, only tackier. I can't read her thoughts anymore, but I imagine they are dark and depressing and involve doing things to nether regions that shouldn't normally be done. I'll second that! I can't believe I ever entertained the thought of getting back with Cass. Was I really that lonely? That hard up?

I watch as a stream of tears start trickling down Brenda's cheeks. She reaches for a handful of tissues and begins swiping at her face angrily. I know she's not crying for me, I know these are tears for her marriage, but I have a sudden, unexpected flutter of sympathy. She doesn't deserve my sympathy, God knows she doesn't. I want it to stop. I want to snigger like I usually do and tell her to "Suck it up, bitch face!" But the sympathy is strong, and there's nothing I can do about it now, so I turn away.

I go looking for Bob.

He's lying on a blue sofa in what looks like the kids' rumpus room at the other end of the house, his eyes shut, headphones over his ears. Whatever music he's listening to, whatever thoughts it's conjuring up, these, too, are no longer open to me, and this time I am relieved.

I don't really want to know if I was an excruciating mother who drove her son to murder. Do I?

Speaking of excruciating, there's mischief afoot, and it involves a pair of obnoxious tweenies, one of whom is clutching a bag of Twisties, a smug look on her pudgy face.

Remember Yana and Eloise from the corner shop? Yes, I know, how could you forget. Well, the little deviants are currently leaning into the police tape like it doesn't exist (what'd I tell you about tweenie girls?) and trying to get the attention of the acne-faced officer.

"We need to speak to the detective guy!" calls Yana. "It's, like, really important!"

The officer looks beyond bored and says, "He's busy, girls. Come back later."

"But it's about Henrietta!" says Yana, her eyeballs bulging.

"*And* who she's been kissing!" adds Eloise, which earns her a dimpled scowl from her accomplice, who clearly wants to be the first to blow the whistle.

The officer is still not taking the bait and says, "This is a crime scene, girls. We haven't got time for gossip."

I'm with Acne Face. That's old news, bitches, get a life.

"But we *saw* them!" Eloise persists as the officer shakes her head and strolls away, towards another officer with whom she shares a patronising smile. *Oh kids*, that smile says, *aren't they just hilarious?*

Na-uh! I want to say. There's nothing funny about spreading idle gossip and wasting police time. There's been a murder here, girls, and my son's love life is irrelevant.

It *is* irrelevant, isn't it? I'm beginning to think so.

Let's move it along because there are more important things to consider, like the fact that Tandia has just found new evidence and she's looking pretty chuffed with herself. Again.

"Spotted this down the side of the TV set in the living room," she says, holding up what looks like a strip of yellow material with a set of enormous tweezers.

Chief is staring at it all squinty-eyed. "What is it?"

"Looks like a headband," she replies. "You know, that keeps your hair off your face."

"Could be the vic's." That's code for victim, in case you don't know. They're talking about yours truly.

"Could be the perpetrator's," Tandia shoots back. "TV was on, gotta make you wonder."

"Okay, bag that one too." He can't muster much enthusiasm, but my attention is now piqued.

I don't wear hair accessories, but I know exactly who does. Perhaps the Terrible Tweenies were onto something.

CHAPTER 23

Henrietta Burleigh has been in my living room. I know this for a fact because, despite her tartish behaviour, she has one simple, almost angelic trademark—a bright yellow headband, which is glued to her hair every single day. I say glued because I have never seen it out. At school. At play. I wouldn't be surprised if she wore it in the shower.

During last year's Christmas concert when she wore a tiger costume complete with full tiger mask (don't ask), she still managed to slip the headband around the tiger's head. I would have scoffed aloud if it weren't for her psycho mother who happened to be sitting two chairs in front.

But here's the thing: as far as I know, before today, Henrietta has never been inside our house. That's partly why I was so surprised when Bob snogged her last week. I've never even known them to do "homework" together (and I use quotation marks there because I might be dead, but I wasn't born yesterday).

So how did her trademark hair accessory get behind my TV set?

Sure, she was due at his sleepover party last night, but that got cancelled, remember?

Looking across at the group of kids now who are still hanging about at the other end of the street, mostly staring into their screens like zombies, I can see that Yana and Eloise are hanging back with Fran, watching it all from a distance, but Henrietta is in the middle of the mob.

And guess what? She is headbandless! Yep, for the first time since I can remember, Henny Penny is missing her yellow headband. Either Henny's been in my living room and dropped it there, or she's chosen a strange day to break the habit of a lifetime.

And if she was in my living room, when was she there? And more importantly, *why?* As far as I know, the only girl who's crossed our threshold in the past few weeks is Fran, and she doesn't wear headbands or not that I know of. I look across. Nope. Hasn't got one on.

Fran's visit had nothing to do with Bob, I should add. Well, not directly at least. I invited her over, not because she's clearly on my side and dobs my son in when he smokes (although that's earned her the key to the city let me tell you that) but because I felt sorry for her. Really sorry.

You know that chick-flick *Working Girl,* starring Melanie Griffith as the uber-haired wannabe? Well Fran's parents look like clones, not of sweet Melanie, but of her co-stars Sigourney Weaver and Harrison Ford—right down to the stiff suits, self-satisfied smirks, and careers that must be worthy of a Hollywood script because they are never home. At least no one's ever seen them there. I have spotted them a few times driving away, both sets of eyes looking straight through me as if deep in thought. They hadn't got to work yet, but it was clear they were already there, and behind them, Fran standing in the driveway just watching, one hand half-raised as if wondering whether to bother.

And what do Fran's parents (do they have names? I've never heard them) do that keeps them so busy? Your guess is as good as mine. We think they must be corporate bigwigs, judging by the gleaming Mercedes and the swanky pile of bricks just up from Junnifer's house (where else?). We're certainly convinced they commute to a larger city. I mean they look way too important to run a business in this dinky-di town, and they do such ungodly hours—depart before seven, home around eight, at least that's according to Yana's dad who was tutt-tutting about it in the corner shop one day. Like he's the model parent.

I know she's around fifteen, but how Fran manages on her own for all those hours I can't imagine. She doesn't appear to have many friends although I hear there may be a housekeeper, again no one's quite sure. There are some older siblings somewhere, apparently. They must have taken off at the first opportunity, and I guess poor Fran is biding her time until she can join them.

Until then, I was trying to give her a family meal and a bit of company. That's why I invited Fran over. I thought an afternoon with Bob would be a treat. Bob thought otherwise, and after a rather awkward hour that included a game of FIFA 16 and some stilted small talk over spaghetti, she headed home and Bob rounded on me.

"Why'd you have to invite *Fran* over? She's not my friend. She's, like, a million years older than me."

"Oh she's about two years older than you, Bob, don't exaggerate."

"Still."

I looked at him pitifully. He was obviously still smarting over that tittle-tattle.

"I was just trying to be neighbourly," I replied. "I know what it's like to be alone."

"No, you *choose* to be alone, that's totally different!"

Sometimes he's eerily like his father.

"We can't all be as popular as Henny Penny," I replied, not realising then how smitten my son had become.

Staring across at Henrietta now, watching as she starts doing clumsy jumps on her board like she hasn't a care in the world, I start to have second thoughts. I mean, why would Henny Penny want to kill me? I'm the mother of the boy she's got a crush on. Surely she'd be sucking up to me so she can suck face with my son, not sticking the knife in?

It makes no sense. It's as ridiculous as the headband in

her hair, or not as the case may be.

Chief must be on a similar wavelength because he is now standing on my front lawn staring down the street towards the kids. He takes a quick glance at the media, who are all busy shoving microphones in my startled neighbours' faces, then says something to one of his lackeys, who scurries off in the direction of the kids.

Within minutes they have been corralled in Cass's yard, out of earshot of the press I suspect. Chief meets them there and holds up the bagged headband. They all freeze. No one says a word, but I can see Henrietta inhale.

"Any you kids know who owns this?" Chief asks.

Silence.

Beside Henny, I see a freckle-faced boy I don't know turn to stare directly at her head with a puzzled expression—*could he be any more obvious?*—but no one offers up Henny's name, and Chasin either doesn't catch that stare or if he does, thinks nothing of it.

"Any of you kids see anything suspicious this morning?" he says now. "Anyone strange hanging around?"

Silence again. Then Sebastian speaks up.

"Actually, now you mention it, I saw a weird guy in, like, a white van with, like, dark windows and stuff."

"Yeah, that's right!" says Freckle Face behind him. "Real creep. He was staring at the house, all creepy like."

"Real creepy," several others echo, and now Chief is staring at them his head cocked to one side.

"You being serious?"

They nod as one.

Chief signals for the acne-splattered officer (has she got a name? I can't remember) to come back, which she does, a jig in her step. She's excited to have purpose.

"Take this lots' statements, thanks Megan (ah there it is!). And feel free to take your time."

Sebastian groans. "But we're goin' to the skate park!"

"Should've thought of that before you mentioned the

creep," was all Chasin had to say, and I get it now.

He does not believe them.

I don't believe them either. I know exactly what they are doing—they're deflecting from Henrietta, and they're using the modern-day monster as a red herring.

What is it with kids and "creepy guys in white vans"? My son has had a fixation with them for the past two years. Perhaps they all saw one in a horror movie once. Perhaps a teacher described one when discussing "stranger danger", who knows? Now whenever some poor bastard happens to drive a white van past a child—any child—he must be a "paedo" (and don't you hate the way kids use that word like a cute nickname, not the horrendous abbreviation that it is?). And God help the poor bastard in the white van if he happens to park near a school or playground.

He will be rewarded with shrieks of "Paedo! Paedo!" like paedophiles don't drive other vehicles in other shades or don't use other means of transport.

This is why I know that even if there was a man in a white van, he was probably just a passing tradesman or soccer dad. But my bet is there was no van. They are covering for Henrietta. Not to mention hindering a police investigation.

The question is, why? What do they know? And why are they protecting a potential murderer because, let's face it, when it comes to the evidence, Henrietta ticks all the right boxes.

Converse sneakers? Tick. Hers are navy blue, but they're close enough.

Blond hair? Tick. Okay, blondish, but we already agreed on that.

Yellow headband? Tick! Tick! An unequivocal tick!

"Er, Chief," comes a familiar voice, and I only just notice the reappearance of the very first cop on the scene. He's stepping out of a police vehicle, and while I'm not sure where he's been, I have a sneaky feeling I know what this is about.

Chief is walking away from the kids and ushering First Copper under the police tape with him and back to the sanctity of my front yard.

"What'd you find out, Johnno?"

"I looked into that AVO like you asked," he tells Chasin. "I've got some more information for you, and you're not gonna like it."

And here I was thinking we'd put that silly affair to bed.

CHAPTER 24

All right then, before we hear what the nosey copper has to say, perhaps I'd better come clean. I might have suggested, earlier, that my affair with Toadface was all his fault, but well, that's not quite the whole story.

Before we go any further, please be warned:

The following material is classified MA15+.
It contains content that may offend some viewers.
Viewer discretion is advised.

Still with me? Great because here's the thing: yes, Todd Karlouis was a total sleazebag who ogled anything in a skirt, but I *may* have taken to wearing skirts in the off-chance I'd be ogled.

Happy now? Have I humiliated myself enough?

I know it's pathetic, but I was lonely, really lonely. That's why I wore short skirts daily, even though I preferred jeans and had no real interest in my boss and they were really quite tricky to work in. You try scrubbing an en suite bathroom in a tight skirt and see how much dignity you come away with.

I just liked the idea of being admired, even by a bloke I dubbed Toadface. It had been a long time since anyone had looked twice at me, and I needed it so badly I took it where I could get it.

So I wore my slutty skirts à la Bridget Jones, and I let

him check me out, basking in the attention but not expecting anything to come of it. Really, my self-esteem was so low I honestly didn't think even a cliché sleaze would try his hand.

And then he did!

It was a major revelation. Somebody wasn't repulsed by the thought of kissing me, which happened in a hot sweaty flourish one day, between the pile of plastic buckets and the vat of Mega Mould Remover. I was caught off guard at first. Call me naïve, but when he said he wanted to show me his "giant Hoover", I honestly thought he was going to exhibit a new vacuum cleaner. And I was kind of excited about that. The old one has never been up to scratch; we really could have done with another.

So I almost slapped him away when his hand went for my butt and his tongue suddenly reached down my throat until a tiny voice inside said, *Steady girl. This may be the only good Hoovering you get.*

And so we tongue danced for a bit before the zips were unzipped and his vacuum cleaner did its biz. Giant it was not, but it still managed to clean me out.

Then, dirty deed over, he grabbed an old mop, told me to wait five minutes, and snuck out. I waited two, reached for a bottle of bleach, and did the same. I'm not sure anyone saw us, we weren't exactly discreet, but I didn't really care. I didn't have a reputation to uphold. Toadface clearly did because the next time he approached me he suggested lunch.

"What for?" I asked.

"Be good to take it out of the office don't you think?"

"What for?" I repeated. I wasn't after a meal. I certainly wasn't after a relationship. I just wanted to liven work up a bit. *That* was the turn-on for me—brief flings between cleaning jobs. And so, five minutes later, I found myself back in the supplies shed being Hoovered all over again.

So, this nonsense lasted, oh, eight, nine months. Not daily, of course. We went entire weeks restraining ourselves, but it was regular enough for the rest of the crew to notice and then, of course, his wife. It was around the end of the ninth month that she accosted me in the car park.

"Are you Lou Gold?" she said, her voice catching in her throat.

"Lulu, actually. Who are you?"

She swallowed awkwardly, waited a heartbeat, then said, "I'm the wife of the married man you've been banging."

After nine months of tongue dancing, I suddenly couldn't find mine and, empowered, she took a step towards me.

"I suppose you think he loves you?"

I shook my head. Definitely not what I had been thinking.

"I suppose you think he'll leave me for..."—she paused to slap her eyes down my body and back—"...for you?"

Nope, wrong again lady. Didn't even want him to.

"Look," I croaked, tongue now located. "I didn't mean—"

"To wreck a perfectly good marriage?" she interrupted.

"Er, no." That wasn't what I was going to say. "I didn't mean for it to go for that long."

She seemed horrified by this answer, and I wonder now whether she was expecting me to fight for him, to say we loved each other and he was mine, all mine! Fact is, as you know, I never even liked the guy. I was just lonely. He was there. That's all there was to it.

"Well, if you ever go near him again—"

I raised a hand like a child in a classroom. "Kinda have to, we work together."

She growled. "Go near him again, and I'll kill you! *Comprende?*"

I felt a little rattled now and pretty pissed off to boot. It takes two to tango, right? So I said, rather stupidly, "Not if

I kill you first!"

That's when her jaw dropped, her skin paled, and I guess she went off and applied for that restraining order. I wonder now what took them so long.

The next day, Toadface called me into his office, looking more sheep than toad, and said the words I knew he would say.

"I'm gonna have to let you go. I'm really sorry, Lulu."

"You know you can't do that," I snapped back, aware of my rights. He was my employer. I could have slapped him with a sexual harassment suit, but the way he, too, paled, the pathetic look on his toady face and the cheque he was now madly scribbling, all quashed my anger.

So I took the money, waved good-bye to my now-contemptuous colleagues and exited stage right.

Two weeks later and just minutes after my murder, the AVO arrived. Too little, too late, lady. I guess Toadface's wife will sleep better in her bed tonight.

Not that Curious Copper says any of this to Chief now. It looks like I spilled my guts for nothing. Turns out the officer knows very little about the sordid affair, only that it ended two weeks ago and Mrs Karlouis applied for the restraining order soon after.

There's one more thing he's found out. It seems that, whatever their anger, whatever their bitterness, neither of the Karlouises could have killed me.

They are 4,500 kilometres away, in Bali, trying to rescue their marriage.

CHAPTER 25

Damn it. There go two perfectly acceptable suspects. Let's cross them off the proverbial list. So where does that leave us?

Back up shit creek, if you ask me, with the Chief holding on to a ridiculous hair accessory. He's now handing it to another officer, one of the early arrivals, the pudgy one with the goatee.

"Take this around the neighbourhood, Paul," Chief says, "see if anyone recognises it. Oh and check with the Joneses while you're at it. There's two girls over there, could be one of theirs."

Officer Paul nods and starts looking around as if wondering who to attack first. I wish he wouldn't bother. We already know who owns that headband, he's on a wild-goose chase.

Paul decides to leave the Joneses for now and heads in the opposite direction, to the weatherboard cottage on the other side of my house, the one in desperate need of a little TLC and some Dulux Weathershield.

I don't really know the guys who live there, a couple of unemployed rednecks judging by the unkempt lawn, the rusty Holden Commodores out the front, and the bad rap music that pumps 24/7. It's always been a cheap rental, and I never bothered to get to know its occupants. What was the point? They moved in and out so quickly I couldn't keep up.

Curiosity getting the better of me, I watch as Paul raps loudly on the door and wait as a tattooed twentysomething with a full beard and a nose ring opens it and looks out like he wonders what all the fuss is about.

Oh hello! Did you not realise there was a murder right next door? That a crowd of vultures have taken over the street? That the media are running riot?

He looks half-stoned and scowls when he spots the officer, probably because he *is* half-stoned. (I wonder if Sarah knows?) Either that or he's the culprit.

I never thought to look in that direction, did I? Now he's got me wondering. Did this stoner stab me to steal some change for his drug habit? It's a bit loose, a bit silly really, but I'm clutching at straws at this stage and I can already tell you he's not going to be much use to Paul. There's no way this dude wears yellow anything or hangs out with anyone who does.

Officer Paul appears to know him—perhaps they've already spoken—and is thrusting the evidence bag towards him for closer inspection. I'm about to zone out when something catches my eye to the side of stoner's house, the other side, the one farthest from my place.

It is like a dark splotch has appeared, a spooky kind of presence. There's nothing over there, no shed that I know of, no reason that area should be closed to me. And yet the darkness hovers, like the Devil's shadow.

I don't want to look at it, I want to look away, but that darkness is distracting and it's sending an icy shiver through my soul.

It is evil, that much is obvious, and it is beginning to freak me out.

CHAPTER 26

Grandma? Grandma! Please come back, please tell me that is not the Devil lurking, trying to lure me down under to the fiery pits of hell. I know I'm not exactly a saint, but surely I wasn't *that* bad?

Or do you automatically go to hell for not believing in it?

I'm not a religious person, never was. Neither were my parents. I'm not even sure they got me christened, they never mentioned it if they did. I certainly don't know of any godparents, and I was never subjected to Sunday school or endless masses, like so many other kids of my era.

But if it helps, I wanted to! You know me, I half envied those brainwashed brats, dressed in stuffy clothes, sitting in a stuffy church, snoring their way through a stuffy sermon (or catching the eye of other kids and trying not to giggle). That just seemed preferable to sitting at home, playing by myself.

I was never indoctrinated with the whole heaven and hell thing, never warned to watch out for Satan or believe God was secretly watching me like a paedo under the bed sheets. Yet there is something decidedly evil about that dark presence which is now chilling me to my core.

Is it really the Devil? Has he come to fetch me? Or is it something else entirely?

A voice whispers in my ear, and I would jump through

my skin if I still had some on. "Don't worry about that, Ludovica, you just need to focus."

Well, hello, Grandma has seen fit to grace me with her presence again.

"Who let you out?" I say and then, "What the hell is that dark evil splotch?"

She shakes her head. "It's not important now."

"Is to me—it's freaking me out!"

"Just take my word for it, Lulu. It's irrelevant, let it go."

Easier said than done. It's still lingering, like a bad smell in a public toilet block.

"Seriously, my dear, you haven't got much time. You mustn't waste a moment."

"All right, take a chill pill. How long *have* I got?" I keep forgetting I'm on a deadline (excuse the pun).

"Enough. If you use your time wisely, just enough."

What the hell does that even mean? I scowl at Grandma. I want to tell her that I am losing patience, the clues are beginning to get muddled up, and I am not sure I am making any progress. Even if I had another twenty-four hours, I'm not sure I can work this thing out, and it's killing me all over again.

But she knows all this already of course and gives me a comforting smile.

"You will get through this, my darling, and you will discover what you need to know. I have faith in you, maybe you need to have a little faith in yourself."

I must not look convinced because she then adds, "Just think of the lovely wish you get at the end of it all. That'll keep you going."

I'd forgotten about that! It does cheer me up.

"Can't I just have it now?" I say. "Can't I just wish to know who killed me and be done with it?"

"It doesn't work like that, and there's a good reason it doesn't because, frankly my dear, that's a pretty stupid wish. Of all the wishes in the world... *really?*"

Well excuse me if I think uncovering a murderer is

important. "So what do I wish for then? *World peace?*"

"You could do worse," she says, then laughs. "Just try to be smart about it. I mean, most people wish for basically the same thing, but occasionally we get some doozies. There's a woman in here who wished to spend eternity with Elvis. We like to have a laugh about that one."

"So is she?"

"Hmm?"

"Spending eternity with Elvis?"

"Well, let's just say she thinks she is. The rest of us know better. I mean poor Elvis, that's hardly fair on him, now is it? There's another guy, oh he's a hoot that one. He wished for an eternity's worth of liquorice."

"Liquorice?"

"I know, right? He was four when he died. Pretty sure he regrets it now." She laughs again.

Yes, death, so amusing. Ha, ha, ha.

"And what did you wish for?" I ask.

She smiles. "Oh I was boring. I wished the same as almost everybody else."

"Which is?"

She smiles wider. "You'll work that out." Her smile drops. "At least I hope you will."

Then she begins to waft back to the light.

"I'm not Miss bloody Universe!" I call after her. "It's not my job to fix the world's shit you know!"

But Grandma has vanished, and I am left wondering what kind of wish most of humanity wants and why, for the life of me, I can't work out what it is.

CHAPTER 27

I take a sneaky peek in the direction of the darkness again but notice it is now moving behind Tattoo Nightmare's garage, almost out of sight.

"Good riddance!" I want to yell and "Ha ha! Scared you off!"

But I'm not sure I can take the credit. Psycho Sarah has returned, from God knows where, and we all know she could scare the scales off a croc. She's standing at one end of the street staring down towards the other, away from the dark blotch, a curious look on her face.

I follow her gaze, and that's when I see her, the one person I thought would be first on the scene. The one person I thought would be sobbing at my gate.

My stalker has finally shown up.

It's the first I've seen of Fiona since this ordeal began, and I'm surprised it took her so long. I honestly thought she'd run down the street, howling, to my doorstep the moment the gossip got out. She's here now except she doesn't look sad so much as, well, *what?*

I can't quite read the expression on Fiona's face, but the way she looks towards her sister, her head to one side, her shoulders hunched as if for battle, seems more like anxiety or trepidation or something.

What exactly does Fiona Palasazuk have to be anxious about?

The two siblings are standing many metres apart,

staring at each other like a Mexican standoff. Except Fiona can't quite meet Sarah's eyes, and I wonder whether she's done something unforgiveable. Is that why she's so anxious?

Did she reward my rejection with a knife to the back?

Sarah is now striding towards her sister, a scowl burrowing into her brow, like a 7.8 earthquake. When she reaches Fiona, she yanks her to one side, and I can see Fiona cower beneath her sister's mighty glower. It's comforting to know even blood relatives are scared of Sarah.

"Why are you here, Fi? What did I say? I told you to stay away."

Fiona cowers. "She was my friend, I'm allowed—"

"*Friend?* After what you did to her? Are you freakin' serious?"

"I didn't mean to hurt anyone. I was in love—"

"Shhhh!" Sarah is glancing around. "Just shut the hell up, okay? Jesus, do you want the world to know? Is that it?"

Fiona shrugs like maybe that's not such a bad thing, and that's clearly not the reaction Sarah wants.

"You disgust me, Fiona. You're not who I thought you were."

"Oh Sarah, I—"

Sarah gives her a look that stills her tongue. Fiona defensively crosses her arms over her breasts.

Sarah glances around again, and something catches her eye. She is looking towards the police officer, Megan, who is questioning the kids.

"What the hell!" she growls again. "They can't do that!" She turns back to Fiona. "I have to go, but I can tell you this, Fi, that was the final straw, I'm done. When you get home, you can pack your bags and piss off. I don't want your kind around here."

What kind? I want to scream. *The murdering kind, is that what she means?*

I never get a chance to find out because Sarah is storming towards the teenagers while Fiona watches her walk away.

She doesn't look anxious so much now as deeply ashamed.

CHAPTER 28

Did my stalker stab me? Is that what this is all about?

Fiona said she loved me, she didn't mean to hurt me. But did she hurt me anyway?

It sounds an awful lot like that, doesn't it? Yet she never wears yellow headbands, she hasn't got black Converse sneakers on, just dusty red Doc Martens, in case you were wondering. And she is not fleeing the vicinity like a typical killer would. Instead, she's standing just metres from a uniformed officer, now chatting casually with two of my neighbours like she's got absolutely nothing to hide.

It's the couple from a few houses down, middle-aged, always smiling like hotel receptionists, just *thrilled* to see your happy face, and how are you today? Except they're not smiling now, they're shaking their heads and wringing their hands and agreeing with Fiona that it's all just so absolutely, completely and utterly *horrendous* (their words, not mine).

Would Fiona just stand there and chat about my horrendous murder if *she* had murdered me? It's unlikely, right? I'm just not buying it, yet I can hear those words again.

"Friend? After what you did to her? …Jesus, do you want the world to know? Is that it?"

Okay, deep breaths. Let's not jump to any conclusions. Fiona's probably just getting her head bitten off for leering at me once too often. This is Psycho Sarah, remember?

She'd smack you down for looking at her twice.

So I'm going to let that one slide for now and follow Sarah instead. She's closing in on the group of kids who are leaning against the side of Cass's house, being questioned by Officer Megan.

"Oi! You! Officer!" Sarah is yelling even though Megan is now looking up and staring directly at her. "What the bloody hell do you think you're doing?"

Megan waits until Sarah reaches her, then says, calmly, "Detective Chasin has asked me to question these witnesses regarding a white van that was seen in the vicinity."

"Not without their parents' permission you don't!" Sarah is still yelling, causing the copper to blanch and the kids to smirk. They're delighted not to be at the other end of Sarah's wrath; no doubt they've been there many times before.

"It's just a few questions, ma'am, we—"

"Don't give a shit. These 'witnesses'"—she's making quote marks, her fat fingers digging into the air like shovels—"are bloody kids, right? You can't just interrogate them! What do you think this is? North Korea? You will have to call every single one of their parents before this goes any further! Got it?"

Megan has regained her colour and looks ready to argue but thinks better of it (I admire her bravery, but she is half Sarah's size) and turns back to the teenagers with a patient smile.

"Right, kids, you heard the woman. You all need to call your folks."

They groan loudly and reach for their phones.

While they're tapping away, I'm sneaking back into Cass's house. Officer Paul has finished with the neighbours (I wish I'd heard what busybody old Mrs Oliver had to say) and is now making his way inside. I want to see how my darling boy is doing and what he's got to say about that headband. If I noticed it on Henrietta from a respectable distance many times, he must have seen it up close and personal at least once.

Paul has managed to gather the entire Jones clan around the kitchen bench, a wide piece of glossy black-and-white marble with leather and chrome stools to match. Tacky don't ya think?

"Do you know who owns this hair thingie?" Paul asks, holding the bagged item aloft for Brenda and her precious little princesses, none of whom are wearing headbands.

Bob goes to say something, his tongue reaching towards his upper palate, when he stops and shakes his head. "Nope."

Paul looks at him through shrewd eyes. He'd caught that too. "You *sure* you have never seen this before?"

Bob shakes his head again, more convincingly this time.

So he's going to defend his girlfriend, hey? Even if it means she killed his own mother.

"Do you think it might belong to your mum for instance?"

Again he shakes his head.

"Know *anyone* who normally wears a yellow hair thing? Or any hair thing like this."

"It's a *headband*, actually, and it looks more like something a girl would wear," says Brenda's eldest, Miss Know-it-all.

Paul turns his gaze upon her. "Any particular girl?"

She shrinks back, blushes suddenly. "No. It's not mine. I'm not saying it's mine!"

Brenda's eyes narrow. She glances at Paul. "It has nothing to do with us," she says stiffly. "My girls don't wear headbands. Hair clips, yes. Headbands, no." She flashes her daughter a look. I can't read it.

Paul glances from Brenda to her daughter and back and goes to say something when his phone bursts into song, breaking the tension. As he steps outside to answer it, the relief in the air feels palpable. Brenda is staring at her daughter shrewdly, and the daughter has her head down not meeting anyone's eyes.

What's going on? Am I reading too much into it? Why is everyone acting so weird suddenly? That *is* Henrietta's headband, right?

I don't get a chance to give it anymore thought because the officer has returned and his eyes are now firmly set on Bob.

My stomach clenches.

"Let's forget this hair thing for now," Paul says, his eyes moving to Cass. "Detective Inspector Chasin has some new evidence in and would like a private word with your son, if that's okay, Mr Jones?"

No! No! Say no! I urge, but he only shrugs as Bob's brow crinkles.

"Right," says Brenda, almost too hurriedly. "Come on then girls, how about we head back to our rooms, hey? This is none of our business now."

She goes to leave, then thinks better of it and turns back, leaning in towards Bob. "Would you like me to stay with you, hun?"

He shakes his head. "Thanks, Brenda. I'll be okay."

Still she hesitates. Then she flashes the officer a chilly glare. "Please don't be too long. I need to get back into this kitchen at some point. I want to make Bob something special tonight."

"Lasagne?" Bob asks, his eyes wide with expectation, and she nods.

"What else?"

Er, spag bol I want to say, but the way he cheers up at the thought of lasagne gives me pause for thought. Perhaps Brenda can't make a decent bolognaise.

She leans down and gives Bob a hug, and this time I watch as he falls into her, and I try not to bristle too much. I suppose he could do with another cuddle. I can't begrudge him that.

Brenda then shoots Cass a worried frown before

following her daughters out of the kitchen and back deep within the house. What's with all these worried looks and surreptitious frowns? Does Brenda's daughter know something? Does *Brenda*? Is she protecting someone?

While Cass and Bob start chewing on their lower lips waiting for Chasin to show, I consider following Brenda, but she's heading back to her bedroom alone. I haven't got time for sympathy, so I toddle on outside. Be good to see what the Burleigh sisters are up to and if there's blood on the streets yet.

No such luck. Sarah has remained with Henrietta who looks mortified as the other kids await the arrival of their parents. Fiona has finished with the middle-aged couple and is now wandering over to old Mrs Oliver, who is leaning on her front fence, looking both scandalised and delighted, like she's watching the Gay Mardi Gras.

Halfway across the street, Fiona glances back for some reason, and something catches her eye. She stops and squints, and I look back too, towards Tattoo Man's house. The shadow has reappeared just to the left of the old sedan.

Can Fiona see that black shadow by the Bombadore? Is that what she's frowning at? And if so, what is this strange phenomenon that only some of us have noticed?

For an exhilarating moment I think Fiona is going to approach it, but then I hear a loud screech, and the shadow suddenly quivers and vanishes completely. I'm not sure if it's been scared off by Fiona or by a sudden ball of bright light that has appeared in front of my house.

It is coming from inside a taxi, and it is shimmering white.

CHAPTER 29

Don't get excited—it's not the archangel Gabriel dropping by to help us out. It's just my mother, stepping out of a cab, and she is very much alive. I'm not sure why she has a kind of radiance around her, but I'm more interested in what she is doing here at the scene of the crime.

Go home, Mum, I want to cry. *You don't need to be here; you don't need to see how I died.*

Dot hands the driver a few scrunched up notes, then shuffles over to the edge of the police tape, just peering towards my front door, tears welling up in her rheumy eyes. She has a walking stick in one hand—when did she get a walking stick?—and a stiff little handbag in the other. She looks a bit like Queen Elizabeth with her tweed skirt and tightly permed grey hair, and now I wish I could help her indoors, lead her to that special chair, the comfy one I was saving for VIPs.

Did I ever let Mum sit in it when she came to visit Bob? Did I ever make her feel that special?

Tandia, who is just stepping out of my house, appears to recognise Mum and strides straight across, a concerned look on her face.

"Mrs Gold?" she calls out. How she recognises Dot I don't know. "I thought we were meeting up at the mortuary a bit later?"

"Yes, pet, I just…" Mum falters. "I just wanted to see where…" She breaks off as her voice catches in her throat.

Tandia reaches a hand out to her across the police tape. "I'm sorry, Mrs Gold. It's still a crime scene. I can't allow anyone in."

She nods. "Yes, yes, of course, dear, I know you have a job to do… I just… I just wanted to be close to where she…"

Mum's knees begin to buckle, and it looks like she's about to fall to the gutter when Tandia grabs her and holds her steady. She glances behind her and motions for another officer, the guy with the receding hairline who has taken over from Megan on boundary patrol.

Together they help my mother across the road to one of Brenda's crisply painted white wicker chairs. I know I keep going on about them being crisply painted but, honestly! You should see them. There's never so much as a mouldy smudge or a string of cobwebs to be found. What does Brenda do? Touch them up every week?

Mum falls into the chair, gratefully.

"I'm sorry, pet," she says. "I shouldn't have come."

"Mrs Gold, you just lost your daughter. You don't need to apologise to us."

"No, but maybe I need to apologise to her."

"Oh?" says Tandia.

Oh? I repeat.

"I wonder now if I had done things differently… If it's partly my fault."

Actually, no it isn't. Listen to me, dear reader, and listen good. My mum did nothing wrong. Both my folks were great. Hell, they were better than great, they were boring, I already told you that. There was no abuse. No neglect. No sticking me outside with a bottle of soft drink and a comic book. They loved me, they provided for me, that's all there is to it. Sure, they didn't give me siblings and didn't take me to Mass, big bloody whoop. Dad's long gone, but I won't let you lay any blame at my mother's feet, and I won't let her either. I don't know who killed me, but it had nothing to do with Dot.

Got it?

"I… I thought we gave her a decent upbringing," my mum is saying. "I thought she knew she was loved."

I did! I do!

"I was so happy when she came back to live here after university. I really thought she'd settle in the big smoke, but she returned! You could have bowled me over with a feather when she showed up one day, bags in her hand, said she was moving back. And we loved having her here, really we did, but she was different, Detective. Something had changed. She became hard. She became brittle. Do you think that's why she was… Why it happened?"

Tandia smooches her lips to one side. "It's early days yet, Mrs Gold. But, well, people don't generally get stabbed unless they make someone very, very angry."

Oh thanks, Tandia, that'll make Mum feel better. Thanks a lot.

"And our investigations seem to suggest that your daughter did put a few noses out of joint."

Dot sighs. "Ludovica could certainly do that, dear. She wasn't always like that you know. She was quite a delightful child. Funny, oh so funny and cheeky like you wouldn't believe. I always thought she'd be a journalist or, heaven forbid, one of those standing comedians."

"Stand-up comic?"

"That's the one. She always found a joke in everything. She was aptly named. After a German king, you know? The eccentric one who built that magnificent Neuschwanstein. Have you ever been to Germany, pet?"

Tandia shakes her head. Mum nods as if she were expecting that.

"It's the most stunning castle you've ever seen. They say Walt Disney modelled Sleeping Beauty's castle at Disneyland after Neuschwanstein, did you know that?"

Again Tandia indicates no.

"Well, anyway, it's beautiful and delightful, and that's what my Ludovica was like." Her face clouds over. "And then, well, she wasn't."

Tandia waits, but when my mum says nothing more, she asks, "Do you know what happened? To Lulu, I mean? Why she became so… brittle?"

Mum thinks about it for a moment. "Not exactly, no." Her lips purse together for a moment. "Although I blame that man. Her first love. He broke her heart. You mark my words, she was never the same girl after that."

The detective is nodding. She thinks she knows what Mum is talking about, but she doesn't have a clue.

My heart got pummelled badly, but it had nothing to do with Cass.

CHAPTER 30

I wish I had time to fill you in. I wish I had time to walk you through the full soap opera of my life, but I don't think it has anything to do with my murder and I just can't hang around listening to Mum telling a virtual stranger what a disappointment I was.

I'm sad that she found me so difficult at the end there, and I'm sorry if I was ever brittle towards Mum. But I told you before, she wasn't responsible for what happened to me, both in life and in death, so this is all a great waste of my time, and yours.

Please, let's stay on track.

Chief Chasin has now appeared and is walking back across the road (who knew a crime scene could be such great exercise?). He is talking into his phone. He is sounding excited for once.

"Okay, got it, yep, great... Yep, yep... Okay, thanks Maurice, I owe you big time."

He clicks off, then frowns slightly as he catches sight of my mother and Tandia on the veranda in front of Cass's house.

"This is Mrs Gold," Tandia tells him, and I watch as his frown softens into a look of polite sympathy. He's a pro, that one.

"I am so sorry for your loss, Mrs Gold."

"Dot, please," she says, taking the hand he is extending.

He glances back at Tandia, the frown returning. "I

thought you were meeting at the—"

"Yes," she interrupts. "Mrs Gold just wanted to be close."

He nods. "If it's any consolation, it would have been instant. Your daughter would not have felt a thing."

Er, actually I did feel a shot of pain before I dropped dead, thanks very much. But I'm quietly glad he said that. Mum doesn't need to know otherwise.

She is nodding, gratefully. "Do you mind if I sit here for a bit? I'll call a taxi in a moment."

"No need, Mrs Gold," he says, reaching for the doorbell. "Tandia can organise a lift for you to the morgue. I wish we didn't have to do the formal identification process but, well, we can't rely on the evidence of a child you see, so…"

Not a child, Detective Chasin, a thirteen-year-old boy on the cusp of manhood.

I can see that young man still perched at the kitchen bench, patiently waiting for the Chief to arrive. He's not having a tantrum; he's not falling apart. Despite finding his mother dead, despite the blood and trauma, he is sitting quietly, waiting, as he's been asked to do. He is filled with dignity.

And I know in that instant that he did not do this thing to me. Bob could not have killed me. I don't care what Chasin has to say or what new evidence he has found. I know that in my heart. I know that deep in my soul.

Bob is innocent.

The front door opens slowly, and Brenda appears to let the detective in, then she spots my mother hunched in the chair.

"Dorothy?" she says, stepping out and reaching down to grasp her arm.

Mum looks up at her, takes a moment to register who it is, then surprises me completely by grabbing Brenda's hand and squeezing it tight.

"Oh Brenda dear, how is Cass? How is poor Bob?"

"They're okay, all things considered."

"The poor child. I can't believe he had to see…"

She nods. "Yes, extremely distressing, but he will be okay, I promise you that, Dot. We will look after Bob, he will be all right." She glances inside. "Will you come in? I'm sure he'd love to see you. So would Cass and the girls."

"No, no, pet, I'm due elsewhere. I'd better not get in the way. This lovely detective is about to find me a lift. I was just catching my breath."

Brenda smiles warmly. "Well if you feel up to it later, please come back and join us for dinner. I'll set an extra place. Just in case."

My mother looks happy to hear this, but I can't help feeling gutted. It's not so much that they get along (who knew they got along? When did that happen?). It just feels as though I have already been replaced. Everybody is moving on. They are having dinner parties without me!

I want to be sitting at that dining room table.

I want to be sharing lasagne with my son even if it isn't as good as my spaghetti bolognaise.

Okay, more deep breaths. Grandma is right. I can't hover here feeling sorry for myself. I need to forge on. Chasin has made his way into the kitchen and is now indicating one of the vacant stools beside Cass.

"May I?" he says.

Cass nods. "Of course, please, Detective."

Oh yes, by all means, wouldn't want you to be uncomfortable while you accuse my son of murdering his mother.

Chief doesn't look excited anymore. He sighs deeply like he really doesn't want to be here, and I wonder if that is the case. It brings me little comfort.

"I've just been on the phone to the pathology lab," he begins, pulling off his glasses and rubbing them with the end of his shirt. He places them back on, adjusts them slightly. "We've got some more information on the weapon that was used."

"The knife?" Cass says, glancing at Bob, and Chief nods.

"Apart from the blood, we located something else on the knife. At first we thought it was mud."

Ah, no you didn't if I recall correctly. I'm pretty sure the word "faeces" was used, and you better not be confirming it as we speak.

He clears his throat. "We found traces of chocolate."

Now he glances at Bob, who looks ready to pass out.

CHAPTER 31

Oh dear, I have a bad feeling about this. Could we go back to the faeces theory instead? Bob must be thinking along the same lines because he is staring stiffly at the wall in front of him, his face like the white cliffs of Dover.

Cass, meanwhile, looks frustratingly unperturbed. He's almost jaunty as he says, "*Chocolate?* Now that's bizarre! Why would there be chocolate on the knife?"

Chief ignores this, and still looking at Bob, adds, "It matches the chocolate cake we found in Bob's bedroom."

His *bedroom?* I stare towards my house, to Bob's room, but it is still not open. It's just a big black blah.

Arrrrghh!

What's that about? He's let me into his thoughts, into his dad's home, but for some exasperating reason, I am still not welcome in his most precious space. It was out of bounds in life, but surely things are different now? Can't he see that?

This rejection cuts me deeply, but I can't worry about that now. I need to keep the focus.

"What chocolate cake?" asks Cass who is anything but focused.

His birthday cake, you moron! What else?

"Hang on," says Cass, grabbing Bob's hands and making him look at him. "You had the chocolate cake in your bedroom, is that what he's saying?"

Bob just blinks. I'm not sure I like where this is

heading.

"Did you take the cake and eat it in your bedroom?"

Bob explodes then. "Why shouldn't I? It was *mine*! It was *my* birthday cake! She made it for *me*!"

"Okay, easy son. Easy."

"No, it wasn't fair! She baked it for me, then she wouldn't let me have it. She said I had been too wicked and I couldn't have it until I apologised! But it was my fucking cake!"

"Hey, watch your language, little man!" Cass says, glancing at the cop apologetically.

Oh for goodness' sake, Cass, we're beyond worrying about a few swear words at this stage!

Chasin says, "So how did the cake get into your bedroom, son, if your mother wouldn't let you have it?"

He is setting a trap, and Bob is falling into it fast. He needs Bob to say the words, "I took it up." He needs to connect Bob to the cake and then ultimately to the knife.

To the murder weapon.

Shut up! I want to scream, but of course I can't.

Luckily Bob seems to have come to the same conclusion because he does shut up. He snaps his lips together, folds his arms over themselves, and looks away. Good boy, I think. Don't say another thing. Be a petulant child again, be a little snot, give them the silent treatment.

Chief persists. "We know the cake was in your room. We found it there, Bob. What we need to confirm is that you also took the kitchen knife up to your room when you took the cake."

Don't answer! Don't answer! Don't answer! I want to scream, but Cass, being a complete idiot, does not attempt to end this conversation or insist on legal representation.

Instead, he asks the detective, "What is all this? Who cares if the cake was in his room? What has a birthday cake got to do with my ex-wife's death? Are you saying the knife that was used to kill Lulu was the same one that was used to cut the birthday cake?"

Oh keep up, Cass!

Chasin nods. "We believe that knife was in your son's possession."

"Believe? So you don't for sure, right?"

Good, now you're getting it.

"We're still—"

"So an intruder could have come into the house, taken that knife and killed Lulu for all you know?"

Chasin looks incredulous. "What? Snuck into your son's room and stole the knife—while he was there—then snuck down the stairs, stabbed your wife, and Bob didn't have a clue?"

"He could have stolen the knife from the kitchen. The intruder. There's stacks of knives in her kitchen, right?"

"Yes, but the cake was in your son's bedroom."

"So?"

"So the culprit would have had to take the knife up to Bob's bedroom, smudge it with chocolate, before taking it back downstairs to stab your ex-wife." Chasin sighs. "Sounds a bit unlikely doesn't it, Mr Jones?"

"Maybe my ex-wife used the knife to cut the cake earlier and dumped it in the kitchen sink?"

Again, great point, Cass! Well done! Checkmate, Detective Chasin!

Even though I know this isn't true. I never cut the cake. I never even attempted to cut my son a slice, but let's keep that to ourselves for now.

Annoyingly, Chasin doesn't buy it. "Sometimes the simplest solution is the best solution, Mr Jones." He looks at Bob. "The cake was in Bob's bedroom. The knife had cake on it. The logical conclusion is the knife also came from Bob's bedroom."

Cass now stares at Bob, who has his hands prayerlike in front of him, hiding his mouth.

"Bob?" says Cass. "Say something! Tell him it isn't true!"

"There's more," says Chasin, and now I really do feel

like I'm going to implode.

Cass mirrors my feelings, his face drawn, his shoulders slumped. I've never seen him look so drained.

"I've just been informed by the lab that a set of fingerprints has been located on the knife, and they don't match the deceased's." He sighs again. "We're going to need Bob to come down to the station. We need to take his prints, and we need to formally question him."

And that's when the world falls out from underneath me.

CHAPTER 32

My first instinct is to run, screaming, towards the tunnel. I don't want to do this anymore. I don't want to know!

Cass may be acting coy or perhaps he just doesn't get it, but I know exactly what Chasin is thinking, and it does not look good for our boy.

Have you worked it out too?

It seems to me that Bob must have returned to the kitchen late last night, after I had gone to bed, and taken the cake from the fridge. He must have grabbed a kitchen knife while he was at it—how else could he cut himself a slice? That explains why the kitchen light was on. It explains why Tandia was holding my dinner plate. It's the one that contained the cake. And it explains why the murder weapon is smudged with chocolate.

I guess Bob went back up to his room and proceeded to scoff the entire cake in defiance of me. I can picture him now, slicing each piece furiously and shoving it in his mouth.

Did he hate me more with each slice? Did he plot my murder with each bite?

Does it really come down to something as trivial as a few cups of flour, some cocoa and some butter? It wasn't even a very good cake if my own lick of the mixing bowl was any indication. I'm a notoriously bad cook. Have been known to burn one dish while undercooking another. I just don't give the recipes enough attention, but I recall now that young Bob never made so much as a complaint. I recall him eating an entire bowl of caramel pudding in which I'd accidentally used salt instead of sugar. He didn't even flinch even though I knew what I had done and begged him please to stop.

He was my champion once. He would have eaten dead cockroaches for me back then. He would have died for me, I know that. When did that change?

When did he start to hate me over something as trivial as chocolate cake?

It doesn't matter, though, does it? Because that must be what he did. He must have picked up that knife, snuck back down the stairs, switching on the TV along the way to drown out the noise, then stabbed me, just the once.

For that alone, I am grateful.

Could Bob live with himself if he had hacked and hacked and ripped me to shreds? At least it was one clean stab, not nearly as haunting. I like to think that he was filled with instant remorse, that he wept over my body for a few moments before he ran out the back door and disposed of the weapon. If only he had managed to get it into the creek, none of this might be happening. They might never have found the murder weapon, or his fingerprints might have been washed off.

You know, that bit has me stumped. Bob always had such a good throw. I wasn't a fan of team sports, but when I watched him hurl a ball, I was always filled with unabashed pride.

I wonder, too, if he sobbed hot tears as he returned to his bedroom, felt anguish and remorse for stabbing me in cold blood.

How long did his remorse last, I wonder?

Was he feeling guilt when he put on that Oscar-winning performance for the first officer on the scene? Or was he already imagining a life full of endless cake and unbridled kissing, free of his suffocating mother?

And what will he think later as they smudge his fingers

into the black ink and shuffle him into a windowless room for questioning. Will he feel regret for doing it or just for getting caught?

Bob is being led outdoors to a waiting police car, Chasin on one side, his father on the other, looking like he's aged ten years in ten minutes.

The reporters have gone ballistic; the cameras are trained on my son. This is none of your business! I want to scream. Just piss off! Leave him alone!

The car door is open, and Chasin puts a large hand on Bob's head. He messes up his hair as he helps him in.

"Hey, watch the hair, Mum!" Bob would cry whenever I tried to hug him to my chest. It was never an angry tone. There was always some humour there.

"Mind your head," Chasin says, and Bob does not say a thing.

I wish I could tell you I'm accompanying him to the station, that I'm hovering over Bob, offering him some kind of psychic guidance, but it turns out there are some unwritten rules I wasn't aware of, like the fact that I can't seem to move beyond a five hundred-metre radius of my house.

They should add that to the rule book. *Thou shalt not leave the place of thy demise.* Or something. Remind me to mention that to Grandma, next time she visits.

I want to follow Bob, I want to shadow him on his journey, but I'm stuck here, bereft. I'm home but I've never felt more lost in my life.

If I had knees, I would have dropped to them by now. I would have buried my face between them, and I would have sobbed my heart out.

Instead, I am staring, dumbstruck, at my old house, my old street, my old life. It is all now as flat and lifeless as a puddle, the crowds dispersing, the last of the media packing up. I am equally as flat (the lifeless bit goes without saying). I have nowhere else to turn. I have nothing left to show you.

I am sorry for wasting your time.

I pick myself up metaphorically and turn towards the tunnel, to the light that is now so close I can touch it. It looks so inviting. It is quivering. It is alive. I can feel its pulse, both oddly invigorating and restful at the same time. The allure is irresistible, and I am very, very tired.

It is time to give up. It is time to step into the—

"Not so fast," comes a stern voice from deep inside the tunnel.

It is Grandma. Again. My God the woman is annoying.

"It's still not over," she tells me, her body now hovering at the entrance. "Keep going, kiddo. You still have time."

"What's the point, Grandma? I know what the truth is now. I don't need to know any more."

"You know nothing, you silly girl," she says, but her tone is gentle. "You're not even close."

Then she looks past me, down to the street where Chasin and Tandia are walking back towards my house, Chasin on his mobile, Tandia looking through her notes.

They did not accompany Bob to the station. Why? Haven't they got their man?

"What's going on?" I ask Grandma, but she has vanished again.

I take a metaphorical breath.

I exhale.

I take another.

It feels like a Herculean effort to move away from the intoxicating tunnel and back to ground zero, like I am wading through wet cement. I don't know what the point is. I haven't got the energy. But something deep inside me tells me I have to go back. Grandma is right; this is not over yet.

Not by a long shot.

CHAPTER 33

The sun is now high in the sky, burning ferociously, and the teenagers have sought shelter under a large jacaranda between Cass's house and Mrs Oliver's on the other side, some sprawled on the grass, some slumped on the weathered lawn chairs.

The tree is the most lurid purple, obscenely pretty considering the circumstances. It reminds me of spring carnivals and taffeta dresses.

Mrs Oliver is offering the kids cold lemonade, which she's presenting in a large plastic jug with matching plastic cups. She has a bottle of heavy-duty SPF 30+ too, but they're ignoring the sunscreen and accepting the drink gladly, as is Officer Megan who is checking her watch and waiting for the final parent to arrive.

I never really got to know old Mrs Oliver (another person I never got to know; so many people, so little time). Perhaps, like the stoner next door to me, I never really tried. She called out to me from time to time, but I rarely stopped to say more than a polite "Hello Mrs O!"

I noticed Bob talked to her often. Did odd jobs for her from time to time. I just saw the old biddy as a nuisance, a sweet nuisance, sure, but one more person trying to steal my son's time.

The final parent is scuttling up now, scowling with concern. It must be Freckle Face's dad because I don't know him, but I can see Junnifer standing behind

Sebastian and Sarah holding on to Henrietta's arm lest she try to escape. There is one other child, a boy with overgrown hair and ripped jeans. Parker I think he's called. His mum is vaguely familiar and has a toddler hitched to one hip. She does not look too concerned. The other kids have all disappeared. Perhaps they weren't necessary? Perhaps they have done a runner.

Megan motions the group to come closer and says, "Okay, then, if we can return to this guy in the van?"

She needn't bother. Chasin is now striding towards them, a finger held up.

"Actually, sorry Officer Megan, I have something more important I need to talk to these kids about."

Megan waves as if to say, "You're welcome to them!"

He pulls a lawn chair up and sits down, waiting until he has their full attention before he speaks. "I need to ask a few questions about last night, and I need the truth now, kids, okay?"

The children all look worried, and Sarah looks fit to burst.

"What's this about?" she demands, and he holds his finger up again.

"Mrs Burleigh," he says almost wearily, as though he's been expecting this. "I could easily do this down at the station if you'd prefer. I can haul the kids in, disrupt everybody's day if you like. Or we could just try to knock this on the head here and now and let everybody get on their way. Which would you prefer?"

It's an unveiled threat, and Sarah looks ready to bite, but I guess even a lioness knows when to retreat, so she just exhales loudly and rolls her eyes. The rest of the group shiver with relief, including the parents.

Chasin turns back to the kids. "I need to know if any of you saw Bob Gold late last night or first thing this morning?"

Now none of the teenagers can look at him. They might well have just said yes.

"Come on, guys," he says. "I'm just trying to help your mate. This is for his own sake."

Nah-uh! I want to scream, feeling buoyed again. What you're really doing is trying to trap Bob, and you're using his friends as bait.

Annoyingly, Sebastian takes a bite. "Might've seen him at his birthday yesterday."

"Oh yes?" says Chasin.

Nuh-uh, I say again. Bob's birthday party was cancelled, remember?

"Yeah we met at the tree house down from the hall. You know just to celebrate and stuff."

The hutch? Really? *When?*

"When was this exactly?" Chasin asks.

Sebastian glances at his friends, frowns and says, "I dunno. Late."

"*Really?*" echo several of the parents, including Junnifer who looks startled and Sarah who looks even more irate. She inhales like she is about to let loose, but Chasin has all five fingers up now, and she slowly exhales.

He says, "Was this after bedtime?"

They nod, the parents pale further. Sarah's eyes are now thin slits in her head. Oh dear, Henny Penny is gonna cop it later.

"You guys sneak out?" Chasin asks, and I have to laugh.

Oh, no, Chief, us parents hold the door open while our kids choof off into the dead of night. *Of course they snuck out!*

Slowly, painfully, he gets the story out. While the parents watch on, apoplectic, the kids tell how they "messaged" each other around midnight and organised to rendezvous at the park.

How my son managed to message anyone without a device I don't know. Or I didn't until Henrietta says, "Bob was really upset. Kept texting sad emojis on his iPhone."

What iPhone?

"He was whinging about what a bish his mum was," adds Freckle Face.

"Jayden!" bellows his dad, but Chasin shoots him a frown.

"Bish?" Chasin says.

Jayden shifts uneasily. "That's code for bitch."

God, even I can work that out. But I didn't know about the iGadget and neither did Chasin judging by his deepening frown. He must want to get his mitts on that now.

"He just needed to unload," adds Sebastian. "So we agreed to meet up you know, to like cheer him up and stuff."

"Who is 'we', exactly?"

Sebastian shuts his lips. He won't dob on his mates.

"I was there," says Jayden, bravely, his father scowling behind him.

"And I was there," says the kid with ripped denim, his mother shrugging as if to say, "Well that figures".

"I was also there," comes the soft voice of Henrietta, and all eyes swing to Sarah. Her jaw tightens, but she does not say a word.

There is another collective sigh.

Chasin nods. "Anyone else?"

Henrietta hesitates, does battle with her conscience, then says, "Just my friend Mary. Mary McIntyre. But she went camping with her folks this morning. I can message her if you like?"

"Not necessary right now," says Chasin, "but I appreciate the honesty. So what did you guys do at this tree house then?"

It's a hutch, people. A hutch!

"Nothing," says Sebastian. "Just hung out. Talked about how shitty life was and wished him a happy thirteenth."

"That's it?" This was Junnifer, and she was not buying it. Her son gave her a filthy look in reply.

"Then what happened?" Chasin asks.

"*Nothing*," Sebastian repeats. "We just talked, that's all! Bob said he hoped his mum choked on his birthday cake, and that was that."

"*Sebastian!*" cries Junnifer, a hand to her throat.

"But he didn't mean it or anything! He was just pissed off with her, like he always is."

Like he always is. Wow. That cuts. Is this what Grandma wants me to hear? Is she trying to rub it in?

"Okay," says Chief. "Did any of you—and I need you to answer honestly again, okay?—did any of you go back with Bob to his house after that?"

They shake their heads emphatically, but he persists.

"Did any of you stay over at Bob's place last night? In Bob's bedroom, perhaps? Or go in there this morning. This is extremely important. I need to know."

Jayden is looking at Henrietta, who is blushing profusely, and now Sarah is looking panicked.

"They've answered your questions, Colin. I think that's quite enough."

I'm more curious about why he is asking this. What has Chasin found in my son's bedroom that indicates a visitor? I mean, if it's just the yellow headband, well that was in the living room, right?

"This is really important, Sarah," the detective replies. "We need to get to the bottom of what happened at the Gold house in the past twelve hours. That's pivotal. And if there's anything these kids know, they need to speak up. It's not just about Ms Gold anymore." He turns his eyes upon the kids. "Bob's future is hanging in the balance."

There is clear hesitation, a conspiratorial glance between them, and then Sebastian shakes his head. It's very subtle, but I see it. I'm not sure if Chasin does. In any case, the kids drop into silence, their eyes suddenly very interested in the flowers that have formed a purple rug on the grass.

Chasin sighs. He looks almost as weary as Cass. "Fine,

if that's how you want to play it." He pulls himself up and turns to Megan, who has been scribbling away on a notepad as they spoke. "If you can finish up here, that'd be great. Make sure you have all their current contact details, and then we can let 'em get going."

"Finally!" says Sarah, but it's purely cosmetic. I can tell she's more relieved than riled. I'm pretty sure Henrietta is in for a bollocking though, but I can't worry about that now.

It seems to me that Chasin thinks one of my son's mates has some information that might blow this case wide open, but why?

Why is he so determined that one of those kids was present at the scene of the crime? Does he think they witnessed something or were somehow culpable?

What else did he find in Bob's bedroom, or does it come back to the evidence we already know about? Let's look at that again.

Is it because of the yellow headband? I can't see why. Even if they work out that it belongs to Henrietta, so what? She's Bob's friend—Bob's *girlfriend* in fact. She could have left it at any time. I'm not around to tell them otherwise. Unless they find traces of my blood on it (which they can't prove yet, surely?), it's evidence of exactly nothing.

Is it the blond strand of hair they found beneath my corpse? Again, it's not exactly a smoking gun. In any case, I just saw the gang, and none of them are strictly blond. Not even Henrietta, whose hair is so much browner than I gave her credit for. As for this Mary girl, the one Henny mentioned? I'm sorry to tell you, I know exactly who she is, and her hair is red and curly.

Chasin can't know about the Converse sneakers, only you and I know that. So what is it then? What is it that haunts the lead detective's eyes as he watches the kids shuffle off, hands shoved in their pockets, heads bowed?

I'm haunted, too, now. Thanks, Grandma. Haunted more than I was before. All I've learned is that I knew my son even less than I thought I did.

He has an iPhone and hides it from me?

He sneaks out of home in the dead of night?

He calls me a bitch and talks to his mates about shoving cake in my face?

Did I really need to hear that?

I'm back on my "knees". Thanks, Grandma. Thanks a bloody lot.

"**O**h, Lulu, what on earth do they want now?"

That's Brenda, and she is swiping at her eyes and trying to fix her face in the hallway mirror as the doorbell rings out. She looks a mess, not quite as beautiful as she normally is, and yet I can't help admire those tears. Her marriage has long been forgotten. They are tears for Bob.

I am touched that she is touched, and I wonder if I have underestimated her. I mean, she should be jubilant, right? Her husband's needy ex-wife is dead, and his son has been carted off to jail. A colder woman might have revelled in that.

I have a dreadful feeling I might have, once.

As Brenda plasters a smile to her lips and makes her way to the front door, I can hear two voices coming from a side bedroom.

"She wasn't that bad you know."

"Who? Mrs Gold?"

It's Brenda's daughters, one sitting cross-legged on her bed, the other leaning up against the side of it, her back to her sister, tapping on her iGadget. My God, can these kids do nothing else with their time?

"Who else, silly?" says the older one. Now what is her name? It's on the tip of my tongue.

"Well I think she was a meanie. I didn't like her very much *at all*." That's the younger one, the one on the bed, whose name also eludes me. How can I not remember that?

"Yes, B," the older one says (Betty! Is it Betty? I don't think it's Betty) "but *Bob* did and that's all that matters. She was, like, his *mum*, remember? She may have been a bit of a meanie, that's true, and, like, she never really had time for us (eye roll at her screen), but she *was* his mum and *nobody* deserves to have their mum die. I mean, gee, imagine how *you'd* feel if *our* mum died!"

This causes B to look shocked suddenly, like it had never occurred to her before, and now her lower lip begins to quiver.

Not sensing this on account of the fact that she's so fixated with Snapchat or YouTube or whatever it is that's turning our children into zombies, the older one (if only I could remember her name) says, "We'd be *sooooo* upset, right?" Tap, tap at her screen. "It'd be like the end of the world, you know." Tap, tap, tap. "My God, I'd just *die!*"

A loud splutter catches the older one's attention, and she glances around at last to see her little sister curled in a ball in the middle of her bed, weeping into her pillow.

The older girl looks mortified and drops her phone like it's a poisoned chalice and leaps across the bed to gather her sister into a hug.

"I'm sorry, I'm sooooooo sorry!" she coos, her own eyes welling up. "I didn't mean to make you cry. Mum's not going to die, we'll be okay, everything will be okay! Mum will be *fine!*"

But B is shaking her head vehemently, and when she finally stops and looks up at her sister through tear-smudged eyes, she says. "I know that, silly! I'm not worried about mummy! I just feel soooooo bad for Bob!"

The older one nods. "I know, it's dreadful! The poor, poor thing! We have to look after him now; it's our job to make sure he's all right."

And suddenly their names come to me in a whoosh. It's Gertrude and Beatrice, how could I forget? I mocked those names once, hell I mocked the girls every chance I got. Not anymore. I have never liked them more than I like them now. Even with their snotty noses and smudged eyes, Gertie and Bea have never looked quite so beautiful as they do at this moment.

CHAPTER 35

I could sit and watch these two cry for my son all day, bless their perfect pink socks, but we really haven't the time. Chasin is now seated back at the kitchen bench, a cup of coffee being placed in front of him.

Brenda is still sniffing, she's not hiding her tears anymore, and he looks at her sympathetically as she sets about making lasagne.

"He didn't do it, you know?" she says reaching for an onion. "He doesn't have it in him. Not Bob."

Chasin just takes a tentative sip from his cup.

She turns back, knife in hand. "It could have been a random burglar, have you thought of that? A rapist who got disturbed? Hell, for all you know I could've snuck back between soccer games—it's only a ten-minute walk away. I had plenty of reason to want that woman dead."

He scoffs, says, "And what would your motive be, pray tell?"

She shakes her head. "Plenty of reasons." She holds up the knife, thinking. "She was always rude to me, how about that? Used to call me NagHag, did Cassowary tell you that? Thinks I nag the poor man senseless."

Brenda *knew* that? I'd blush if I could.

"It's nonsense of course. Lulu thinks... *thought* that chatting to your husband, actually having a conversation that lasts longer than 'Pass the salt, please' is somehow nagging. The thing is Cassowary and I could always talk about anything for hours on end. He loves that we communicate; that's what drew him to me in the first place."

Chasin gives Brenda a "yeah right" look, glancing down at her lovely long legs as he does so, and she shakes her head emphatically.

"It's true! He just needed someone to talk to. God knows he barely got a sentence out of Lulu after the baby…" She shrugs. Lets it drop. "Anyway, the point is, I could very easily have snuck into her kitchen and stabbed her myself!"

She pokes the knife in the air to drive home that point.

I am surprised by this revelation but also touched that she is throwing herself in front of Bob's bullet.

Chasin seems more amused than anything else. He tilts his head at the knife. "What? Past thirty-five other parents, kids and their coaches? We checked your alibi a long time ago, Mrs Jones. You didn't kill Ms Gold. But good try."

Wow, okay, I didn't know that, but I'm surprised to find myself relieved. I never really stuck to Brenda as a suspect, but it's still good to know she's in the clear. For all her sins, she was a good mum. I could never take that away from her. She needs to be off the hook, she needs to be home with her girls, and she needs to be there for my Bob. Who else is going to make him his favourite dish? Who else is going to make him lasagne?

Bea and Gertie could promise the earth, but it's a mother Bob needs now, and a good one. God knows I wish it was me, God knows it breaks my heart, but in my absence, I know that Brenda will make a decent run of it.

I just hope Cass wakes up to himself and recognises that before it's too late.

Brenda is now smashing up some garlic and takes a few minutes to stir it in with the sliced onion and some mince before glancing at the detective and frowning.

"So why aren't you back at headquarters then? Interrogating the poor boy?"

She's so much smarter than her husband, that much is now obvious.

"How did your daughters get on with Ms Gold?" It's a random question, comes out of nowhere, and she frowns at it.

"Fiiiiine," she replies slowly. "What's that got—?"

"And Bob?"

"Sorry?"

"How do your daughters get on with Bob?"

"Great, actually." She sounds defensive. "They're great mates. Especially Bob and Gertie. Very close." Her frown deepens further. "I really don't see what—"

"I'm just trying to get the lay of the land, that's all."

She sniffs. "Well, we might not be *The Brady Bunch*, but we all got along just fine. No major hiccups. Everything as it should be, I can assure you of that, Detective."

"And yet there's still a few things that don't add up."

A flash of anxiety enters her reddened eyes. "Like?"

"Like where your husband was all this morning. That's the bit I keep coming back to."

The anxiety drops back a notch. "So now you're after Bob's dad?"

He shrugs. "Gotta wonder, though, don't you? I know it's been playing on your mind."

She sniffs again, but I'm not sure if it's just from cutting the onion. She stirs the mixture, then reaches for a can of tinned tomatoes. "I *was* wondering that," she says eventually, "until I got over myself and realised it's beside the point. I mean, it's all a bit trivial, considering the circumstances."

She shoots him a look.

"So you're not worried he was with someone else?"

The look intensifies. "Listen," she says, "Cassowary may be unfaithful, I guess that should surprise no one, least of all me, and I certainly don't expect any sympathy. But I can tell you this. It is completely irrelevant where my husband was or who he was with this morning, because

Cassowary is no killer. Couldn't hurt a fly." She smiles sadly. "I mean that literally. Whenever there's vermin to be caught, cockroaches to be squashed, he can't do it. Has to get Gertie to do it for him would you believe?" She half laughs. "She's the gutsiest member of this family. Cassowary? Nope. Doesn't have it in him. Not a mean bone in his body."

"That's not what Mrs Oliver says."

We both look at him surprised. Has old Mrs Oliver been talking out of school? Does she have it in for Cass?

"According to your neighbour, your husband has a cruel streak, Mrs Jones. She says he used to flaunt his affair in his ex-wife's face." He frowns a little, looks almost embarrassed. "She said something about him conducting the affair with the lights blazing. Can you tell me what she means by that, exactly?"

Brenda says nothing for a moment, then does something neither Chasin nor I are expecting. She bursts into peals of laughter, buckling over and clutching her stomach like it might explode she's laughing so hard. It feels incongruous considering the circumstances, obscene even, and I feel my old anger return.

What's so damn funny about Cass flaunting his affair in my face?

Why is that something to be laughed at?

Brenda shoves a hand to her lips as though trying to suppress the giggles. She holds the other hand up and waves a palm at Chasin. "I'm sorry, sorry," she says, straightening up, calming herself down. "I didn't realise Margie saw that! How embarrassing!" She takes a deep breath. Lets it out again. "Cassowary wasn't flaunting his affair, Detective. He was sending out an SOS."

"Sorry?"

She laughs again, but there is no joy in it now; it is mirthless. "Cassowary thought I was completely clueless, like I had noooooo idea. But I knew. I knew what he was doing." She smiles sadly again. "He was trying to catch her attention. It was a cry for help." And then because Chasin still looks bemused she adds, "Despite my best efforts, Cassowary always wanted to keep the curtains open when we made love. Said something about needing the fresh air, but I knew what he was up to, and I didn't blame him for that, honestly I didn't. He wanted Lulu to see us. He wanted to get caught! He wanted her to march on over and haul him back home like a naughty little boy."

"And this didn't worry you?"

"Well of course it *worried* me, Detective, but there wasn't a whole lot I could do about it. I loved him. Still do." She turns back to the chopping board. Starts hacking at a carrot. "Despite what Lulu thinks"—she catches herself, sniffs, amends her words—"*thought*, I never wanted to destroy her marriage. I had fallen for Cassowary, but I wasn't out to hurt her." She glances at the kitchen bench. "It all started out so innocently, with cups of coffee right where you're sitting, just chatting, nothing dangerous. He just needed somebody to talk to. He never directly criticised her, but I knew he was deeply unhappy. I also knew he loved her very much." Her glance wanders towards the road. "I could tell by the way he would get up and linger near the window, looking back at his house, hoping she'd look up and cross the street, pull him back out." She sighs, then starts slicing a zucchini. "When that failed, he tried loud sex. And I knew what he was doing. I let him do his silly dance. I let him try to get her to notice."

Brenda stops and stares at the bright red splashback on the tiled wall in front of her. "I always thought he should have been called Raggiana."

Now Chasin looks doubly confused. As am I.

"I don't know why his folks named him after the Cassowary. He's more like a beautiful bird of paradise, like the Raggiana." She turns to the detective. "Papua New Guinea's national bird? Extraordinary creature, exquisite orange and yellow and green feathers, long black tail wires. They do this amazing dance, showing off for their mate—

madly clapping their wings, shaking their head." She closes her eyes, sways a little. "He used to do that for me once. I'm not sure when it stopped..." She opens her eyes and gives herself a shake as if it does not matter, then resumes chopping again. "But that's what he was doing back then. That's what Margie Oliver is talking about, bless her heart. He was dancing for Lulu. Clapping his wings in the window, hoping she would come swooping in and haul him back to their nest."

Brenda scrapes the vegies into the pan, puts a lid on top, turns the gas down, and then pulls a stool out from the bench.

"Despite it all, Detective, Lulu didn't seem to care. For twelve months she just ignored it all like it wasn't happening, then suddenly, *finally*, she threw him out. She released him to me." She smiles sadly again. "It took me another four years and two babies to convince him his rightful place was here." Her face clouds over. "But lately..."

"Lately?"

She frowns. "Well, I thought he was doing his dance for Lulu again. Turns out it was for someone else. I guess I got that one wrong. And I guess I never did understand how Lulu could watch him prance about in front of her eyes and ignore him for so long. It took her ages to kick him out. How could she stand it? I don't think I'd have the patience. I don't think I'd have the *strength*. Was she taunting him, do you think? Was it payback? Did she not care?"

She seems genuinely stumped by this, and Chasin has no answers for her, but I am left reeling, gobsmacked, in fact. Brenda has it all wrong, or at least part of it.

Oh Cassowary, if only you knew. I wasn't ignoring you for twelve months. I wasn't taunting you or getting my revenge. It's worse than that, so much worse.

For twelve long months I never looked up. I never looked out. I never even noticed you dance.

CHAPTER 36

Chasin and I both leave Brenda to her cooking and her memories, and he wanders back to the crime scene, while I dare a glance towards the tattooed guy's house.

The dark shadow is nowhere to be seen, but I have spotted two princesses of darkness walking along the road, towards the skate park.

Did I tell you there's an old skate park on my street, halfway between the corner shop and the cul-de-sac? It's just a graffitied concrete quarter-pipe built back in the early '90s. It's since been superseded by a whiz-bang new half-pipe near the village hall, so you rarely see anyone other than "babies" using it. I know Bob and his mates would never be caught dead there, weaving their boards between the five-year-olds and their anxious dads. Yet there they all are.

Well, all of them it seems, except Bob. Oh, and Sebastian, who's just making his way there now from the other end of the road. He must have dashed home to get his board, which he's dragging with one hand while the other holds his mobile phone.

Yana and Eloise are close behind, trailing him, listening in as he speaks.

He says, "Yeah, I couldn't believe it either. It's like she's lost her marbles or got something on her mind or something. She just said, 'Whatever. I'll be around if you need a lift.' Like nothing happened!" He laughs. It's more of a scoff. "I know, right? I thought they'd all go frickin' mental. Even Henny's mum! Couldn't believe she kept her cool. Henny reckons she hasn't said a single word about it. Reckons that's worse! It's like all the adults have had personality transplants or something." He pauses as someone says something, then laughs again. "Yeah, yeah. Okay, well grab your board, see you there… Nah, not at the tree house, retard. At the old skate park. Yeah… yeah I know it's lame, but we want to stay close, right, you know, just in case…"

He doesn't finish that sentence, simply clicks off, but I wonder what he means. Why is he staying close? What's he waiting for? What's he afraid of?

Sebastian shoves the phone into the back pocket of his jeans and drops the board to the road to start skating when the tweenies close in.

"We saw you kissing her, you know!" says Yana, a smarmy smile on her lips, which have a smudge of something bright orange on them. Twisties, I think. It undermines her authority; I wonder if she knows that.

He turns, stops, frowns in her direction. "What?"

"We know you've been sexing with Henrietta!" says Eloise.

Is she getting her facts muddled up again?

Sebastian doesn't seem too fazed. He rolls his eyes slowly at her. "It's not sexing, you ugly slag, it's just makin' out, and anyway so what, she's my girlfriend."

"Na-ah, she's *Bob's* girlfriend."

"*Na-ah*," he mimics. "She was just faking it, and you two got sucked in. Like everyone else."

Really? Why would she do that? Why would Henrietta fake a kiss with my son? What would be the point?

The tweenies don't think to ask these vital questions, they simply glance at each other looking flummoxed while he steps onto his board and pushes off down the street.

As Yana and Eloise burst into absurd giggles, Sebastian glides towards the skate park where at least ten other teenagers have congregated. I want to follow. I want to hear what he has to say. I want to know why Henrietta was fake kissing my son.

But my head is completely muddled up. Just an hour ago Bob was telling me, secretly, in his thoughts, that he kissed Henrietta to scare her away.

"I should never have kissed Henny. I only did it to scare her off."

Now Sebastian is saying Henrietta was the one faking the kiss.

What are these kids playing at? Who is scaring whom, exactly? And when did childhood romances become so bloody complicated?

CHAPTER 37

You know, I never had a boyfriend at school, so I don't know how these things work. I never had a childhood sweetheart of any description, which probably won't surprise you. But I did go out with a boy *from* school, after the trauma of school was done. So I guess we were childhood sweethearts in a sense. We were only nineteen, although we never fake kissed anyone else just to scare the pants off each other. At least I didn't.

His name was Ashton Bailey. We got together at university. He was studying business, and I was just filling in time with an arts degree. I never really had any ambition or none that I could articulate.

He was a handsome, gangly-looking bloke with a mop of golden hair and a cheeky, lopsided grin. He'd never even looked twice at me at school, so I was shocked when he sidled up to me one day while I was shuffling from a history tutorial to a politics lecture and said, "Hey, wanna catch a movie later?"

I remember glancing around, behind me, to my right and left.

He laughed and said, "They're playing *The Rocky Horror Picture Show* at the Pickhouse Flicks at midnight. You look like you'd be a lot of fun to watch that with. What do you say?"

I said yes and the rest, as they say, is history. We fell madly in love or at least went a little mad for eighteen months until we broke up.

But I digress.

I don't want to think about all that now, the what ifs, the what might have beens, the future that never eventuated. There was a lot of water under the bridge between Ashton and Cass, and I'm not sure any of it is relevant.

I want to focus on two thirteen-year-olds who may or may not be going out, who may or may not have led my son on a merry dance. Who may or may not know something about my death.

Were Sebastian and Henrietta having an affair? Were Bob and Henny? Who's telling the truth here? Who is lying? Can you even call a relationship between two thirteen-year-olds an affair, especially if all they're doing is swapping saliva?

It's too silly for words. I just can't see any of it leading to murder.

Perhaps Brenda is right. Perhaps the kids weren't deflecting after all. Perhaps it really was a random stranger in a white van with shady tinted windows, who wears Converse.

You haven't forgotten the Converse sneakers, have you? I'm looking carefully, and I can tell you that almost every kid gathering at the skate park right now is wearing that particular brand. What pathetic clones they all are. What a pity individuality went the way of handwriting and good manners. If it hadn't, we might have sewn this up hours ago.

But here's something we did forget. I can't believe we were so stupid (no offence or anything). We never checked if *Bob* was wearing his Converse sneakers when he came out of his room this morning. We know he was dressed in yesterday's clothes. He obviously hadn't bothered to get changed when he snuck back from the hutch last night, but I can't remember if he had shoes on. We never checked his feet when he walked into the kitchen or later when he opened the door to the police. We never got to see if there were splashes of my blood all over them, a crumb or two of chocolate.

Is he wearing them now? You know I can't see, but you've got to wonder, are they currently being bagged for evidence, or are they still on his bedroom floor, hidden beneath piles of sweaty clothes and tangled computer cables?

I give his room a cursory glance, I don't know why I bother, when I realise something is different. My heart leaps with joy. The roof has lifted, and I can see straight inside!

For the first time since my murder, Bob has invited me in to his inner sanctum.

CHAPTER 38

Whoa! Hold your horses, people! Back up a bit. Let's not rush in, all guns blazing. I realise Bob wants me to see now, and it's very decent of him I'm sure. Wherever he is, whatever's happening to him, he is imploring me to get in there and have a rummage. I love that, really I do, but I'm not sure I have the energy for this.

I'm not sure I have the courage.

Can I ask you a favour? Can you take a quick peek? Can you tell me, are there photos of me with my eyes hacked out? Is there a journal spewing with venom, a sketchpad depicting my demise, or a laptop with Google entries like, 50 Ways to Kill Your Mother?

Is my name written in chocolate icing across the back wall?

Okay, calm down, Lulu. You're getting hysterical. All of that is not important now. What's important is that Bob has invited me in, and so I must enter.

I inhale deeply, I brace myself, and I step over the threshold into my son's life.

It's been a long time since I've been in this room, too long by the look of all the cobwebs and dust. Is that a crusty piece of pizza under his bed? We haven't had pizza for months.

And where are his Scooby Doo posters? He used to live for Scooby and Shaggy. Now his walls are covered with pictures of Taylor Swift and sports cars and towering basketball players doing insane slam dunks. Does he even like these things?

I never knew. Just like I never knew he liked lasagne or had an iPhone or was battling over a girl with his best mate.

But surely that's not important now. Surely that's not what he wants me to see. Surely this goes deeper than LeBron James and pop music.

But what am I looking for?

I notice his bed is unmade. No surprises there. And I notice black crumbs on an old maths book on his desk. That must be where he placed his birthday cake. The one I denied him.

My God, is there any more potent symbol of my mistakes than that silly bloody cake? Did he really stab me over it, and if he did, can I really blame him?

It was *his* birthday cake for goodness' sake! I baked it for him. What was I thinking holding it to ransom, teasing him with it, refusing to let him have so much as a nibble?

Had I let him have it, would I still be alive today? Do I even *deserve* to be? Because I know it's not really about the cake. It's about the fact that I tested him daily. I tested his love even though I never found him wanting. I handed him puddings made of salt and denied him Sundays with his mates, and I made him a birthday cake knowing full well I would not let him eat a single slice.

What kind of mother does that? What kind of *monster* had I become?

My mother's only half-right. I wasn't just brittle. I was a bish.

And to think it all started over one little kiss and a cigarette. How stupid and irrelevant. These are the things that make life worth living—silly kisses and sneaky ciggies.

They are life's chocolate icing.

No wonder my son looked at me so viciously this morning. No wonder he stormed back to his bedroom after I told him to move out. It's little surprise that he grabbed that cake knife and returned downstairs to thrust it into my back.

Maybe it was a spur-of-the-moment thing. Maybe he was blind with rage. Either would be preferable to the idea that he went back to his bedroom with the sole intention of retrieving that weapon and slaughtering me.

But if he did, I honestly can't say I blame him.

I shake myself out of my pity party and keep looking about.

Focus, Lulu, focus.

Where would you hide evidence? Where would your deepest secrets be stashed? I swoop down to look under the bed and am rewarded with two of the most beautiful objects I have seen all day—my son's black Converse sneakers. They are sitting, strewn below his bed, yesterday's socks still squashed inside. They are not muddy, they are not chocolatey and they haven't got a drop of blood on them.

Oh thank you, thank you!

Is this why Bob asked me inside? Is this what he needed me to see? It's a pity they're no proof of anything to anyone but me. Chasin never knew about the Converse sneakers I saw as I hit the ground. I was too dead to tell him, remember?

Hang on, what's that at the other end of Bob's bed? There, on the carpet, in a huddle? It looks like an old blanket, one of the spare ones I keep in the crate behind Bob's door for when Sebastian sleeps over or the temperature drops. What's it doing lying on the floor, and why is there a pillow beside it?

Oh, right.

Now I get where Chasin was going with this, why he interrogated the kids. Bob clearly had a visitor last night. A sleepover. One he was ashamed of, or he would have asked me. Wouldn't he? Maybe not. I was a monster, remember?

I have another sudden flash of memory, this one about three or four weeks back. These memories are coming thick and fast now, aren't they? Do they have a purpose?

I am reading a book, and Bob is staring at me, strangely.

"Mum?" he is asking, his voice wary.

We hadn't been fighting back then. This was before the illicit kiss. Before I knew anything of Henny.

"Yes, darling?" I replied, keeping my own tone light, my eyes still fixed on the book in my lap.

"What would you do if you ever found someone sleeping in my bedroom, you know without permission? One night?"

I glanced up. "Someone?"

He glanced away. "You know, like a girl or something." He glanced back, barely able to meet my eyes, but I didn't think anything of it. He was testing the boundaries, trying to work out what's what.

I laughed and said, breezily, "I'd kill you first, then hunt her down and chop her into tiny pieces. Why? Planning on inviting a girl over are you?"

He looked stunned, shook his head. "No, no, 'course not!" Then all but ran from the living room.

I remember sniggering at that, thinking, *Good try, bucko* and simply returning to my book. I can't even remember what I was reading, but I wish I'd paid him more attention. I wish I'd taken him seriously. I wish I had said, "Is there something you need to tell me?" or "What's going on, Bob?"

Now as I stare down at that blanket, I have to wonder. Was he intending to invite a girl over? Did he invite Henrietta into his bedroom? Or someone else? And what, if anything has this got to do with my death?

I am willing the blanket to talk to me and then it's like it does, because I realise now that I have it partly wrong.

Whoever slept over did not share the bed with Bob. They slept on the floor, alone. Why else would the blanket and pillow be down there?

Chances are it might not be a girl then.

This fills me with relief, but it's not the best bit. I don't really care now whether my son was sleeping around or whether he had a mate back without permission. That's just irrelevant.

What consoles me is the realisation that whoever slept over also had access to that knife.

CHAPTER 39

No wonder Chief was questioning those kids. No wonder he was pressing them on which little piggy slept where. He's no idiot. He, too, has seen that blanket and put two and two together.

This is a good thing. This is hope.

Maybe Chasin realises that it wasn't my son who killed me but his secret guest?

Chasin is still lingering, you know. He must be due back at headquarters, but something keeps him here. There is something on his mind. He is now standing in my bedroom, a messier, less frilly affair than Brenda's. More *Secret Hoarder* than *The Bold And The Beautiful.* He is staring at the picture frame by my bed, the one of Bob and me at a beach somewhere. Our faces are clenched together, our arms wound tight around each other. Bob must be eight or nine in that picture. That's the last time he let me hug him like that.

"Come on, Ludovica Gold," Chasin says aloud, "talk to me."

Oh, Colin Chasin, I wish I could.

"Did your son stab you? Was he capable of that?"

No, I want to tell him. A thousand times no, but I can't prove otherwise and the evidence looks grim.

Then he says something else that sends a shiver down my spine. He says, "Maybe Bob had a partner in crime, hey, Lulu? Maybe he was in cahoots. Maybe someone did it for him to help him out."

Oh God. Maybe he's right.

Maybe that blanket doesn't absolve my son so much as give him an accomplice. And an accomplice means premeditation. And premeditation means life.

And so I am forced to reevaluate the suspect list again. I am forced to sift it down to the people he is most likely to invite back to his room. The kids. And to two kids in particular.

They both have Converse sneakers on, and one of them owns that headband.

Let's look at Sebastian again.

He's a beautiful-looking boy, Master Cloak, did I tell you that? Prettier than Henrietta and certainly better looking than Bob. Rich kids tend to be attractive, why is that? Must be something to do with superior diets or doctors or the fact that Daddy hooked up with a pretty flight attendant or model or PR girl, because when did you last see a rich guy choose a dumpy checkout chick?

While Bob had a kind of cuteness to him, Sebastian was exquisite—tanned skin, chiselled cheeks, a devilish glint in his green feline eyes. Even at such a young age, it was clear he would grow up to be a lady-killer, if he wasn't one already (yes, I know, it'd be funny if this wasn't so serious).

I had never known Sebastian to fight with Bob, certainly never seen them have a scrap, but I had witnessed him argue with his mother many times. He frequently sneered at her, stormed off regularly, he even called her the C-word once.

It was quite shocking at the time.

The boys were only ten, we were all at the local swimming pool, and Junnifer had arrived to take Sebastian home. He didn't want to go. He was having too much fun.

"Come on, Sebby," she'd said. "I've got to get home, get some washing on."

"Well go do it then!"

"Don't be rude, please. Come on, it's time."

"I'm not going, so you can piss off you…!" I'll let you fill in the blanks.

Junnifer, of course, was gobsmacked and didn't quite know what to make of it, so she pretended she didn't hear him and said simply, cheerfully, through gritted smile, "I'll be in the car, Sebastian. You've got two minutes."

But I saw her turn away. I saw the brutal blush on her cheeks, like she'd been slapped in the face with a shovel. And I saw the wobble in her step as she made her way out.

I wanted to step up then. I wanted to yell at Sebastian and tell him to get the hell out of the pool and go apologise to his mother, but something stopped me. Something made me look away.

Was I enjoying Junnifer's discomfort, was that it? Was it the fact that something wasn't going perfectly for her for a change?

And why would I think like that? How did I decide that life was a bowl of roses for her, that she needed punishing? Sure, Junnifer had a better car and a nicer house, and she spoke with a plum wedged firmly in her mouth. But she was still a single mum like me, right? She was still struggling to make it all work, and I'm not sure, now, that the model of your car or the size of your backyard or the way your voice sounds makes a jot of difference.

I never told you before, but she also works full time. She's a real estate agent. Fits, doesn't it? Works six days a week, in fact, which is why she wasn't at the pool with the rest of us that balmy Saturday. She'd been showing houses all day and looked utterly exhausted when she'd arrived to collect her son. Junnifer has no partner or ex-husband across the road to share the load, yet she always manages to find time to bake cakes for school fundraisers and drive kids to Bouncy Bounce and collect her son from the local swimming pool even though he lives walking distance away.

Unlike Fran's parents, for instance, Junnifer… no, *Jennifer* managed to juggle a hectic career and still make her son feel cherished. So why was I so hard on the poor woman? What was that about? Perhaps the C-word would have been better directed my way.

I guess that's beside the point. What we need to ask is, if he'd speak so harshly to his mother in public, would Sebastian raise a knife to me in private?

Would he do it if Bob asked him to?

Did Bob ask him to?

I can't get my head around that. Or is it my heart that's refusing to see?

What about Henrietta Burleigh?

She's now crouched at the edge of the quarter-pipe watching Sebastian do tricks on his skateboard, her long brown hair flopping over her face, no longer restrained by a headband. I can't quite see her eyes, but I can see her lips, and they are sloped downwards.

I'm as surprised as Sebastian that Sarah has let her out. After today's revelations, I expected Henny to be grounded for life. Is that why she's sad, because her mother is also acting weirdly? Or is she crying for Bob? Is she wishing she didn't deceive him with his best friend? Or worse, help him kill his mother?

Sebastian comes to a rattling stop at the top of the pipe, then grabs his board with one hand, sweeping it up before dropping down next to Henrietta.

"You okay?"

She shrugs. Chews on one nail.

"You can't keep beating yourself up about it. What's done is done."

"But it's all my fault."

Oh God, I think, oh God, here it comes.

Sebastian has pushed his board away and now has one arm around Henrietta, the other taking her face and forcing her to look him in the eyes. It seems like such a grown-up move, almost tender. I almost look away.

"You didn't know, Henny," he whispers. "We weren't to know that would happen."

"But if I hadn't kissed him…"

"It doesn't matter now. Let it go."

"But what if he gets arrested. What if he goes to jail?"

"He won't, you'll see. It'll all be fine."

She doesn't look convinced. "Do you think? Do you think he'll tell the truth? Do you think he'll dob?"

Now it's Sebastian's turn to look worried. "I don't know."

Then he takes her in his arms and kisses her clumsily on the lips, and she kisses him right back.

Oh dear, it's just as Yana and Eloise said. These two are most definitely a couple. There's no denying that. So where does that leave Bob? Why does Henny regret kissing my son, and who should he be dobbing on?

Did these two have something to do with my murder? Is Bob covering for *them*?

I am as confused as I ever was.

CHAPTER 40

I want to keep a beady eye on these two traitors. I want to see what else they say, but I can hear a mobile phone ringing back at my house and it feels urgent, don't ask me why. It just sounds shrill and panicked, like the voices in my head.

Chasin snaps it up quickly. He doesn't hesitate, doesn't even say hello, simply barks, "Give it to me!" and pauses while he listens.

Whatever is said, it's short and sweet, and the detective clicks off, looking pensive. He turns to Tandia, who is seated on the stairs again, just near my front door, scrawling something on an evidence bag.

"Not the son's," he says, and she looks up.

"The prints?"

He nods. "No match."

Yes, yes, YES! It's the best piece of news since my murder. I am happier than I have been in hours.

Tandia, too, looks relieved. Her trademark smirk has vanished. She smiles ever so slightly. I'm not quite sure about Chasin yet, but it's clear Tandia, for one, wasn't gunning for my son, and I am grateful for that.

"So where does that leave us?"

He doesn't say anything at first, but I have a great answer for him. "Up shit creek"—I want to sing—"without my innocent son!"

"So let me get this straight," Tandia says. "We have a

bloody murder weapon, complete with chocolate icing. We have evidence that it came from Bob Gold's bedroom but no evidence that Bob Gold actually touched it."

"He could have wiped his paw prints off, of course," says some bozo cop who's been leaning on the banister, listening in.

The senior officers scowl at him.

"Then there'd be no prints on the knife, Phil," says Chief. "Or at least smudged ones. Forensics tell me there's a pretty clear set."

"Oh right. Sorry." Bozo looks away, pretends to be very interested in the balustrade.

"Doesn't mean he wasn't in it with someone, didn't conspire with someone else to kill his mum," says Chasin, who's back to the accomplice theory. "Maybe he put one of his mates up to it."

Now why did he have to go and ruin the mood?

"Explains the blanket," agrees Tandia. "Maybe they plotted and planned all night and then he watched as… whoever… killed his mum."

Come on, Tandia, I thought you were on Bob's side.

"So we need to source that set of prints," adds Tandia, and Chasin nods. "Do we have the ex-husband's on file?"

My ears prick up.

"You think *they* were in on it together?" That's Chasin. He appears to give this some thought and is happy with what he comes up with because his eyes begin to dance. "I suppose they could have conspired. Sounds like father and son were both well and truly over meddling mum. Maybe Bob was in his room upset about the birthday party and crying to his dad, and maybe Mr Jones had finally had enough."

"Grew a set of balls," adds Tandia.

Chasin nudges his eyebrows up. "Maybe he saw the knife on Bob's desk and thought, bugger it. She's killing this poor kid. She's got to go before she destroys him completely. It certainly fits with what he told me."

I shudder. It does, doesn't it? It fits almost too perfectly.

Did Bob call his dad after he stormed off to his bedroom this morning, on his illicit iPhone no less? Did Cass come to my home while I was making toast? Did Bob let him in, or does Cass have his own key somehow? I wouldn't have seen him enter because the kitchen door was shut. Did he go up to Bob's room and see how distraught the poor boy was? Did it force him to grab that knife and dash down the stairs and stab me to death, to free his son at last? And is Bob covering for him now? Is that what he's really sorry about?

"Oh, Mum, I'm so, soooooo sorry!"

But what about Jennifer? Wasn't she in Cass's bed this morning? Isn't that what we decided on? If so, she was either fast asleep when he snuck out, or she's covering for Cass as well. Maybe *that's* why she's still hanging around! Because she knows the last person to enter my house this morning was her lover, and she's battling with her conscience, wondering whether to dob! And maybe that's why Sebastian looks so worried. He's worried for his mother.

"So how does that explain the blanket on the floor?" says Tandia, throwing a bowl of cold water over everything. "How do we explain that?"

Good question, I suppose, but Chasin doesn't think so.

"Could be irrelevant. Could've been left there from a previous sleepover. I mean when did your kids last put their shit away? Tidy their bedroom floor?"

She blows air through her lips. "Yeah, you've got a point." She squints. "So what do we do now?"

"We stop making guesses, and we start finding more evidence, starting with those fingerprints. They're the key. They're the answer. We need to round everyone up and start eliminating suspects. Starting with the husband." He turns to go. "Oh and those bloody kids. I don't know about that blanket, but they're hiding something. They're not fooling me. They're protecting someone, and I thought it was Bob, but now, well, now I've got to wonder."

He reaches for the door handle.

"Where you off to, Chief?" Tandia calls out.

He doesn't turn around as he calls back, "Time to head to HQ and see what Cassowary Jones has got to say for himself."

Sadly I can't hear what Cassowary has to say, he's out of earshot, remember? But I can overhear two women gasbagging in a nearby backyard.

A croaky voice says, "She had a lot on her mind that one. Too much for one little lady, that's for sure."

Great, one more person to tell you how horrendous I was. I look across. It's Margie Oliver. I wondered when we'd get around to Cass's elderly neighbour.

She's in her backyard again, under that lurid purple tree, a flouncy hat on her head, a glass of lemonade in her hand, the pitcher nearby. It's like a bottomless jug.

She's chatting with Fiona, who is not packing her bags as instructed but lounging on a lawn chair beside Mrs Oliver as if she hasn't a care in the world. Personally, if Sarah told me to pack up, I'd already be in the next shire.

"How do you mean?" Fiona asks.

"I could just tell, Lulu had a lot of worries, a heavy soul. Never did find out what she was so depressed about. But you mark my words, love, she was not a happy camper. You could see it in her eyes. Flat, you know? Lifeless sometimes."

Fiona nods, staring into her glass. "You got that right, Mrs O. I liked to bring her muffins, something to cheer her up. She worried about her kid too much, that's what I thought. Always worried he'd get hurt or in trouble or something."

"Don't know why, dear. He's a good kid that Bob." She leans towards Fiona, drops her voice. "You don't think *he* did it do you? They're not looking at him for it are they?"

"Hope not!"

She leans back. "Nah, he couldn't've done it. Loved his mum too much, talked about her all the time. Told me how much she sacrificed for him."

He did? I can't tell you how comforting those words are at this stage, like cold running water on third-degree burns.

"Yes, he's a good kid that Bobby boy," Mrs Oliver continues. "Of course she kept him on a tight leash, which helped. You have to these days, don't you? Kids run amok if you don't. All on their silly little phone thingies and never bothering to say please or thank you. But Bob's different, he was one of the good ones, not like that snooty friend of his, Sebastian I think they call him. What kind of a name is that for a young Aussie lad?"

"Oh Sebastian's okay, Mrs O," Fiona goes to say, but the older woman is having none of it.

"He's got airs and graces that one, right little shit if you'll excuse my French. 'Entitled' I think they call it. Thinks the world owes him a living, and the way he speaks to his *mother*! You wouldn't read about it! Certainly wouldn't get away with that nonsense in my day. Not Bob though. Oh no, love. He was a good lad that one. Always polite, never raised his voice to his dear mum, not the once. Came and mowed my lawn each fortnight, did you know that?"

Fiona shakes her head.

"Well he did, and he'd only take ten bucks for it. I tried to give him more, but he said, no, I needed it more than he did. Sweet, darling child. All her doing, you know. Nothing to do with *him*." Her face nudges next door, towards Cass's house. "It was *her* that spent all the time on the boy, wouldn't take any crap. I know people say she was a bit, well, prickly, but she was never prickly with me, never got a rude word out of the lady. She minded her own business and I minded mine, and that was fine by me. I sensed she was sad, but she didn't let that get in the way of her parenting. I could tell she was bringing Bob up right. I can't fault her for that." She pauses, leans in again. "You don't suppose Bob did it, do you? He couldn't have could he?"

Fiona stares glumly into her glass. It's empty.

"Can I get you another one, dear?"

"No, no, I should get on, thanks, Mrs O," Fiona says, probably anticipating an afternoon packing boxes. She places the glass on the lawn table and stands up, thanks the old lady for the drink and turns to go.

That's when she sees something that makes her frown.

I follow her gaze, and I see it too. The black shadow has returned, hovering like a giant blowfly, a little closer to my house.

"I knew it!" she says. "I thought that was him!"

"Who's that, dear?" Mrs Oliver is asking, but Fiona is already making her way across the road and towards the dark blob. Whatever that shadow is, whoever's inside, it is not scaring her the way it scares me. Her frown has turned into a radiant smile.

She stops at the edge of the shadow and laughs. "I thought that was you! It's been so long! So you heard about poor Lulu then? Come on, let's hug it out."

As she reaches out her arms, the darkness dissolves, and in its place stands a flesh-and-blood human being, one with lanky limbs and hair of gold.

I knew I had sensed a dark presence! I knew there was something lurking here that didn't want me to see. It's Ashton Bailey, my first love.

I would have preferred the Devil.

CHAPTER 41

I mentioned Ashton, right? The boy I met at uni. Did I also mention we were soul mates. I'm not sure I did.

I know it's corny, I know it's trite. The adult me would scoff at that. But back then, back at university after we sniggered our way through that silly movie, I was smitten and so was he. It was instant.

Don't listen when he tells you otherwise.

While everyone else was doing the Time Warp, he whispered sweet somethings in my ear, reached for my breast and clenched my heart at the same time. We were drunk on love. It was like a poison, a hallucinogen, like crack and ice and heroin in one. Better than any silly movie or silly dance.

I just had to look at him and I was giddy, shivering with excitement. He was my first love, my only love. He was the man I was going to marry.

And then suddenly he wasn't.

"I think we should slow things down a bit, hey Luz," he said to me one day about eighteen months later while in my dorm room as I was readying myself to go out. We were heading for a cheap meal somewhere. It didn't matter where, I just wanted to be with Ashton, seated across from him, staring drunkenly into his eyes.

Turns out he wanted to be anywhere but.

"Maybe we should, you know, call it quits, hey babe?" He was so matter of fact about it, like he was debating whether to get pizza or a curry.

I remember it vividly. I was looking in the mirror at the time, the mascara brush at one set of lashes so I was forced to see the horror that flooded my eyes.

"What?" I said, waiting for the punch line. Praying for a punch line.

He sounded flippant. Infuriatingly so. "Sorry, Luz, but this is getting too serious for me. We're too young. Don't you think?"

No I did not think, and I told him as much over and over for the next three hours where we stayed holed up in my room, our hunger forgotten, him trying to escape, me refusing to let him out until we talked it through. Until I talked him back.

"What's happened?" I implored. "Did I do something wrong? Tell me, please, I promise I'll stop doing it."

And then, "Maybe you're just tired. We could just try a few days apart? I could manage that."

And then finally, "Oh my God, you've met someone else!"

"No, no, it's not that."

"It has to be! Who is *she*?"

"I promise there's no one else," he said, and that felt worse than if he'd agreed. Because if there was no one else, why not me?

Eventually he managed to get me away from the door and pulled me to the bed and made me sit down. "I really am sorry, Lulu," he said, "but I'm exhausted by all this." He waved a hand directly at me. "I just need a bloody break, that's all."

Like I was a full-time job.

Then somehow, at some stage, we were naked and making love, and it was like it never happened. And I remember waking the next morning thinking, *Oh thank God, that was only a nightmare* only to find he'd taken his toothbrush and fled.

He never got stuck in my room again. He made sure of

that.

"I had to come," he is now saying, staring back at my house.

The press have left, the police tape is unravelling in the wind, and most of the crowd have grown bored and headed home.

"Heard about it on the news, couldn't believe it when they said it was Lulu Gold. Had to see it for myself."

"I know," Fiona replies. "Unbelievable, huh?"

He does not nod. That's not what he means. "They know who did it yet?"

She shrugs. "Don't think so. God, I still can't get my head around it. Who would want to hurt Lulu? Who would do such a thing?"

He murmurs something. She glances at him, her eyebrows raised, and he says, "Just sayin' I'm not *that* surprised."

She raises her eyebrows farther, and he lifts a bony shoulder in response.

He is still thin, still rakishly good-looking. He hasn't changed a bit. It's like our breakup never left its mark, never etched itself into his being the way it etched into me. I wonder if he is married? If he has kids? If he ever found his real soul mate, the one who didn't feel like hard work.

"Sorry," he is saying, "but she could be so infuriating. I can almost see someone wanting her dead."

"Ash!" says Fiona, bless her heart.

"I know you shouldn't speak ill of the dead, Fi, but she gave me hell for a long time there, you know that. I never would've come back here if she was alive. I couldn't risk her seeing me in case it all started up again. I think I'm only just realising she's really gone, that she's not coming back, that I'm free. It's only when I saw your face that I knew it was true. That I felt safe again."

Ah. That explains why he was hiding in that dark shadow then. The coward.

Fiona tilts her head. "I think you're exaggerating a bit there, Ash. She wasn't *that* bad."

"Maybe, but you weren't there. She got real freaky on me. Bit stalkerish for a while there."

"She loved you, man, you broke her heart, you know."

He snorts. "You think I don't know that? She told me as much every friggin' day for weeks and months and years even. Letters, phone calls, came to my workplace once, begging me to take her back. We'd been broken up for *three* years! It was ridiculous. Embarrassing!" He tilts his head to one side, frowns a little. "And then suddenly it just stopped."

Fiona turns to look at him directly now. "When? When did it stop?"

"I don't know, thirteen, fourteen years ago. I was so relieved."

She smiles knowingly. "Yeah well that adds up. That's when she finally met Cass."

"The husband?"

"Ex-husband now. Cassowary Jones."

He nods, but I am not nodding. Oh no you fools, you have it all wrong. That's when I finally had Bob.

CHAPTER 42

Something shifts again. I am barrelling backwards. I am seated at my kitchen table, across from Cass, a pot of coffee between us. Coffee, it's the recurring motif, have you noticed that? I have just finished ranting about our son and his "abominable" behaviour, his smoking and kissing, and how he could bloody well move in with his father the second he turned thirteen. It is the last conversation I will ever have with my ex, and he is smiling idiotically, like I have just told a lame joke.

It pisses me off. "What are you smiling at?" I'd railed. "It's not funny, Cass!"

"I know, sorry, Lulu. But… well, he's a good kid, you know? A really good kid."

I wanted to slap him about for that, but I knew, even then, that he was right. "Yeah, of course I know that. I'm just trying to stop him from going off the rails, that's all."

"He's not going to go off the rails, Lulu. He wouldn't dare, not with you as his mum! You go on about Sarah, but geez, you're the scary one!"

He'd laughed, and I had scowled at first and then, begrudgingly, laughed along. I didn't think he was serious, but now I have to wonder.

"Do you remember when Bob was little?" I said. "He was so sweet, wasn't he? Couldn't even lie properly, just couldn't tell a fib. I caught him once, when he was about three, scribbling on the wall, and he owned up immediately. Thrust the crayon at me and said, 'I done it!'"

I smiled at the memory, but Cass was no longer smiling.

"How could I remember that? You didn't let me near him."

I slapped him playfully across the arm. "Yes I did."

"Nope." His tone was still deadpan.

I scowled then. "Well, you did walk out, remember? You deserved it."

His smile returned suddenly, which caught me off guard, and he said, "I'm talking before then. When he was a youngster. It was like you and him against the world. I never got a look in."

"Oh string up the violin. So, what, that excuses you for slipping off for a bit on the side?"

"I wouldn't have done it if you had given me the time of day."

I snorted. "I was breastfeeding a needy baby, Cass."

"Baby?" He laughed. "He was a boy."

"Couldn't've been. I was still breastfeeding when I kicked you out, remember?"

His smile vanished. "Yes, and Bob was four."

I had forgotten that I breastfed that long, but I wasn't about to apologise for it. "I was doing what was right for my child. I was looking after his health."

"No, Lulu. You were keeping me at arm's length, and you were looking after yourself."

So kill me. Bob filled a gaping hole in my life that Ashton Bailey created. So what? I had tried hard to fill it many times over, with university and work and, too frequently, various versions of Toadface. But nothing did the trick.

It's not easy to patch up an aching void with total shit, you know? It appears to do the job, but it's actually quite porous—you can smash it in with one putrid kick.

I gave my heart completely to Ashton Bailey, and he

destroyed it with barely a second glance. It took me years to get over him. I guess my heart refused to lend itself out again.

Poor Cassowary, he never stood a chance.

And then Bob came along.

Cass is wrong about that, by the way. I didn't deliberately bait for a bloke. It wasn't a sperm donor I was after that night in the Irish pub, at least not consciously. I just wanted to fill the void, albeit momentarily again.

I had no idea Cass had fallen for me. I certainly hadn't fallen for him. My wounded heart made sure of that. I wasn't about to fall for anybody. I was done with *soul mates.*

Then I fell pregnant, and the world suddenly shifted on its axis. At first it filled me with horror. My initial instinct was to storm into the Commonwealth Bank branch where Cass worked and smack him around the head with the urine-soaked home pregnancy stick. But I didn't. I took a deep breath, had a calming cup of coffee (yes, bloody coffee!) and gave myself a chance to think.

That's when I realised this could be a good thing. This could be a positive relationship. It would be different to the rest!

As I massaged my flat stomach, I began to see that this baby was a part of me. It wasn't separate. It couldn't break up with me the second it got bored. This was *my* child, *my* cells, *my* inner being. He would love me unconditionally, how could he not? He came from deep inside. *He* was my soul mate.

Suddenly I was prepared to give my heart away again because I wasn't really giving it away, I was giving it to a part of me. I knew then that my child couldn't help but love me forever, no matter what happened.

And he did, didn't he? Even though I gave him plenty of cause to despise me like Ashton, even though I was the most suffocating of mothers, he did love me, I know that. He still loves me now, despite everything. I can feel it.

And he needs me now more than ever. And I need you.

I need you to help me help Bob.

Forget why Ashton dumped me or how I fell pregnant or why Cass walked across the street and into Brenda's bed. None of that matters now, don't you see? We need to give this one final push, one final effort to uncover exactly what happened for the sake of Bob.

For the sake of my one true love.

CHAPTER 43

A desperate wail shakes me from my reverie, and you're probably glad of that. I've been getting lost in memories haven't I? Getting a little too philosophical and distracted. It's time to get back to earth again, back to the street between my house and the nearby skate park because there's something big going down.

The kids are all standing on the road now, next to a police vehicle, and in the middle of them all is Jennifer, clinging on to Sebastian like he's about to head to the gallows.

"Please, madame," says Officer Megan, one hand on the open car door. "We're asking for all of Bob's mates to be fingerprinted, not just your son."

Jennifer is having none of it.

"I know what you're doing! I'm not stupid, you know!" She turns to seek out Sarah, who is rushing towards them, fists like Cornish pasties at her side. What are they both still doing here? Are they just hanging around, waiting for the drama to unfold?

"They're trying to incriminate our kids, Sarah! They're trying to pin it on them!"

"What's going on now?" Sarah demands, causing Megan to seek shelter behind the car door.

"We're just asking, please, if all the children who met at the tree house last night could please present themselves to the station sometime today for fingerprints. I'm just offering the kids a lift, that's all, but we're not saying it has to happen right this second. Just at their earliest convenience."

"What the hell for?"

"Detective Chasin wants to eliminate them from our enquiries."

"Incriminate you mean!" says Jennifer.

Megan takes a deep, calming breath. "It's just procedural, please ladies. If they didn't do anything, they have nothing to hide."

"*Do anything?* Of course they didn't *do anything!* They're just kids for Christ's sake. What are you going to charge them with? Break And Enter of a Tree House?"

Chasin is just driving past when the furore breaks out. He growls to himself, then pulls his vehicle over and calmly steps out, glancing around him as he does so, and I know what he's looking for. He's double-checking the press have not returned. He doesn't want this caught on tape.

I can't see any cameras, any starchy hair or bad Italian suits. I think they're in the clear, and I feel his relief. The shouting is causing a few neighbours to look outside though. A few start wandering up.

As Chasin approaches, Sarah turns her wrath upon him. He is the only one I have ever known not to flinch at this. He looks almost amused. Now I wonder whether they have any history. Did they go out once?

Sarah says, "Colin, I won't have this! I won't have you try to pin it on our kids! *Everybody* wanted to stab that bloody woman, you can't just blame our kids."

Thanks, Sarah, nice of you to say.

Chasin sighs. "Nobody's trying to pin anything on anyone, Sarah, you know that. We're just doing our job."

"Pissy fuckin' job you've got there."

His nostrils flare. He's not amused anymore. "Listen, Sarah. We have a set of prints on the murder weapon that we can't find a match for. I repeat—the *murder* weapon.

What do you think I should do with those prints? Hm? Ignore them? Pretend they're not there?" She blinks back at him but says nothing. "We know for a *fact* that someone else slept over in the Gold house last night, so someone else had access to that knife. We need to know who that was. And all we're getting from everybody is lies, lies, lies."

He's getting quite heated now, staring out at the gathering crowd, which includes Ashton and Fiona who are wandering up. The smiling couple are also watching, smiles frozen on their faces. It's the most animated I've seen the top detective all day, and even Sarah seems taken aback. But Chasin's not finished yet.

"I don't care whether you liked Lulu Gold or hated her, frankly that's not the point. That woman was murdered this morning, *in cold blood.* Somebody took a knife and stabbed her in the back. Somebody knows something, and *everybody* is telling me lies! That's all I've been getting since I got here this morning, and frankly, I'm jack of it!"

He's glaring at the group as a whole, taking a moment to stare at each shocked face in turn. Some are meeting his eyes, some are looking away. The couple are no longer smiling.

"Now, we could all just pretend it didn't happen, keep lying to the police, covering up the crime, or we could cut the bullshit and start telling the truth. Somebody killed a woman in this street this morning, and it's my job to find out who that somebody is. And I don't give a flying toss whether the victim was Miss Congeniality or not! She didn't deserve that but she does deserve some bloody justice!"

Everyone is suitably shamefaced, but I am feeling chuffed. Chasin really is my champion. I get that now. All he wants to do is get at the truth, no matter where that leads and who that lands in jail, and I have to admire him for that. He takes a moment to let his words settle in before lowering his voice and turning his attention back to Sarah and Jennifer.

"Now, as I said before, we have a suspicious set of fingerprints that we need to account for. Maybe they belong to one of these kids, maybe not. *Hopefully* not. But I won't know until I eliminate them from my enquiries. It's nothing personal, it's just procedure."

"Well, I'm sorry about Lulu, really I am," ventures Jennifer, her tone still haughty, despite Chasin's tirade, "but it had nothing to do with my boy. He was home with me all morning. I can vouch for that."

Chasin looks at her wearily. "Is that a fact?"

She nods furiously. "Yes. Yes it is. I saw him in his bed this morning. He slept in late. It must be one of the other kids."

It is a mistake. She regrets the words the moment they are out, shoots a wary look at Sarah whose jaw has set tightly again.

Sarah turns her dark look upon Jennifer. "*Really* Jennifer? *You* saw Sebastian in bed this morning did you?"

Jennifer shrinks back and says limply, "Yes?"

"So you were home then, were you? All night and all morning?"

Jennifer stares at her with imploring eyes. "Yes!"

Sarah goes to say something, all eyes now upon her, but then stops and simply shakes her head, folds her arms, and glances away. Jennifer almost crumples with relief. It's like she's just missed a bullet. She breathes deeply, catching her breath, when her son steps forward and clears his throat.

"Ahh, no you weren't, Mum," he says, his lips curling into a grin. "You went out last night, remember?"

"I... I don't know what you mean, Seb," she stutters, blushing various shades of pink. "'Course I was home."

"Nah. I checked when I got in, but you weren't in your bed. I figured you must've slept over somewhere, like the other night. Checked again this morning, Mum. Your bed wasn't even touched."

Busted! There's no denying it now, Jennifer. It's just as Sarah said. You were sneaking about at some ungodly hour having your ungodly way with Cass!

Except… Hmmm… The timing's all wrong. She couldn't have been at Cass's last night because Brenda and the girls were there. This doesn't quite add up.

As Sebastian's grin morphs into a sneer, I look at Jennifer and my heart plummets. I am suddenly back at that public pool, staring at a woman crushed by the words of her son. Her cheeks are a brutal beetroot red, and she looks as though he has belted her across the face again.

If it's possible for an entire suburb to go deadly quiet, then that's what's just happened. Not a mower is mowing, not a car revving up, not a cow mooing in the nearby paddock. Just an eerie silence as the eyes dart from Sebastian to his mother and back.

Chasin looks furious again. "If I recall correctly, Mrs Cloak, you informed my officers that you were home all night and only left a few minutes after the homicide took place. Do you want to explain yourself? Would you like to amend your statement?" He's nodding at Megan who grapples for her notebook.

The colour in Jennifer's face is now draining away, less beetroot and more turnip suddenly. "This is madness!" she cries. "Why would I want to kill poor Lulu? Why?"

"No one's saying you killed Lulu," Sarah spits back. "But don't go pointing the finger at Henrietta, right?"

"I wasn't pointing any fingers. I was just saying Sebastian could not have done it. He's a good boy. He wouldn't have!"

Sarah snorts at this and looks away again, but Chasin is not done yet.

"But you can't possibly know that if you weren't home, can you, Mrs Cloak? So where exactly were you this morning? Where were you when the homicide took place? And no lies this time."

Silence has returned, and you can almost hear the tar road contracting in the cooling air as Jennifer stares sullenly at Sebastian's feet. He's looking very confused now, almost apologetic. He'd enjoyed catching his mum out, it was a favoured pastime, but he wasn't having so much fun anymore. He didn't like where all this was heading. It was just meant to be a joke, so why was everyone looking at his mum like she's a serial killer suddenly?

"Just tell them," comes a soft voice from the crowd, and Jennifer seems to shrink into herself.

I look around. Who spoke? The voice is familiar, but I didn't quite catch who it was.

Jennifer also looks up, a hand to her throat, a desperate look in her eyes. "Please," she says to no one in particular. "Not in front of…" She glances at her son.

"Come on then, kids!" Sarah suddenly booms, making everybody jump. "I'll take you down to the station, get this over with." She points at Sebastian, Henny, Jayden and Parker. "You lot, follow me. Car's back at my place. And hurry up, I haven't got all day! The rest of you can piss off back to the skate park!" She goes to walk away, then stops and turns back to the startled children. "What are you waiting for? A friggin' invitation?"

Teenagers scramble in all directions as Sarah shoots Jennifer a look I have never seen before. There's a slim smile on her enormous lips, and her eyes are soft and conciliatory.

Jennifer offers her a relieved nod in return, then does something I would never have pictured her doing twenty-four hours ago. She drops down onto the side of the road, squatting in the gutter, her knees up, her arms wrapped around herself.

Shaking her head from left to right, she eventually whispers, "So kill me, I spent the night with someone. Who really cares?"

Then she looks up and out towards a face in the crowd. Chasin and I follow her gaze and do a double take. She is staring at a woman.

She is staring at Fiona.

CHAPTER 44

Okay, hands up who didn't see that one coming? Well, maybe you did. Maybe you're quicker than I am. But it's still got to knock you for six, right?

Here I was thinking Fiona had the hots for me, and it turns out she was having her merry way with Jenny in her granny flat two blocks away! I have to laugh at my own folly. How smug was I? How egoistical and vain, thinking Fiona was stalking me, when all she was really doing was hanging around in the hope of running into Sebastian's mum.

The conversations I overheard this morning are beginning to make more sense. Sarah must have caught them at it, which is why she was chastising first Jennifer then Fiona.

"You think I'm going to let you get away with your disgusting behaviour in my neighbourhood?"

"You disgust me, Fiona. You're not who I thought you were."

Sarah wasn't talking about my murder at all but a rendezvous between two lovers. I was so preoccupied, so narcissistic, I never saw that clearly.

Chasin doesn't seem nearly as scandalised as everyone else, more disappointed than anything else. He has a quiet word with Megan while several onlookers watch openmouthed, including Ashton, who is staring at Fiona like he no longer recognises her.

For her part, Fiona looks unapologetic. She is shrugging, blowing air up at her fringe.

"*That's* why you kept hanging at Lulu's so much!" says one half of the middle-aged couple, and Fiona's smile deflates.

"No, it wasn't! Well, maybe initially. I mean, it was a good excuse to see Jen when she dropped Sebastian over. But no, I told you before I liked Lulu. I might be one of the only ones, but I did. She knew I was queer, and she still invited me in for a cuppa." She meets their glare. "It's more than you ever did."

The couple frown and look away.

Fiona drops onto the sidewalk beside Jennifer. Nudges a shoulder at her. "You okay?"

Jennifer sniffs and raises her eyes to the heavens. "How long do you think I've got before it's doing the rounds?"

"Hmmm… Fifty, maybe sixty seconds," says Fiona, and they both snort, trying to restrain a laugh.

This causes the couple to huff loudly and walk away.

"Good riddance!" Fiona yells out after them, and Jennifer giggles like a schoolgirl beside her.

Chasin steps back and nods his head in Megan's direction. "You're going to have to give your statement again, Mrs Cloak. And let's try to tell the truth this time, hey?"

His tone is still dry, but his anger has subsided, and she grins back stupidly.

She says, "The truth, the whole truth and nothing but the truth?"

"So thank you, God!" adds Fiona and they fall about laughing.

Okay then, we might just leave those lovebirds to it. They've gone a bit silly, haven't they? I can't say I blame them. It must be quite intoxicating, releasing a pent-up secret to the world, although I'm not sure why it had to be that way. They're both single, both adults, why not just meet in the cold, hard light of day?

Were we all so judgmental that they couldn't face us?

I guess Jennifer was protecting Sebastian, Fiona protecting Sarah and Henrietta, but from what? Seems a bit unnecessary in this day and age. It's silly what we do, sometimes, in some misguided belief we're protecting our loved ones from, well, *life*.

Fiona and Jennifer's relationship is no one's business, really, although if I'd known, if I hadn't been so delusional, I might not have wasted so much time and energy thinking of them as suspects. And when you think about it, there goes a potential witness too. No wonder Chasin looks so downcast, because if Jennifer was with Fiona this morning, then she could not have been with Cass. She cannot testify one way or the other whether he snuck out of his bedroom and murdered his ex-wife.

This leaves both Cass and Bob out in the open. They're more exposed than they've ever been, and the truth seems as elusive as the waning light.

CHAPTER 45

As Megan starts scribbling down Jennifer's revised statement, Chasin returns to his vehicle and finally makes a clean getaway. He's looking relieved, but I don't know why. He's going to have his hands full down at the police station, which must be bursting at the seams about now.

He has Bob. He has Cass. He has Sebastian, Henrietta, Jayden, Parker and Sarah. That's a lot of people to question. That's a lot of fingerprints to check.

He's going to be there for hours, and sadly, we don't have time for that. Grandma is calling to me again from the entrance to the tunnel. She has one finger in the air, and she is waving it about. Let's hope that means I have one hour left, not one minute. I give her the thumbs-up.

Okay, dear reader, it's time to get our skates on. It's time for a final recap. It seems to me we've been labouring under several false pretences, which have now been blown out of the water. No more assumptions. No more wild guesses. Will you take a moment to go through the facts with me?

The Facts As We Know It:
At 9.25 this morning, I was stabbed. By someone wearing some kind of dark-coloured sneakers. Maybe Converse. Maybe not.
The kitchen light was on, as was the living room TV.
The back kitchen door was open. The internal kitchen

door was shut.

The murderer used a large knife, the same knife that was used to cut my son's cake.

He/she may, or may not, have dropped a blond hair in the process.

He/she may, or may not, have left a yellow headband behind.

He/she may, or may not, be in cahoots with my son.

My son never touched that knife.

See, that's the really interesting fact, if you ask me. That last one. If Bob didn't touch that knife, who did? Who wrapped their fingers around that blade's handle and plunged it into my back? Who is even capable of doing such a thing? Are children?

That's what Chasin seems to be insinuating, but I can't get my head around that, really I can't. I still think we need to look at the adults. They're the only ones I can picture doing something so horrendous, but who do we have left?

Our suspect list is now very malnourished.

We know Brenda didn't do it or Jennifer, Fiona, Todd or his wife. Their alibis are all rock solid, but Cass's alibi has been shattered. If he wasn't in bed with Jennifer this morning, was he there with someone else? Brenda seems to think so, but I'm beginning to doubt it.

Brenda's "evidence" is pretty flimsy. Reeking of coffee is not quite lipstick on the collar now is it? So where was Cass this morning? Was he really asleep in bed, alone or otherwise, or was he in my home, commiserating with my son, plotting to get rid of me?

That's another of Chasin's theories, but there are plenty of other suspects, you know. He's not the only one without an alibi.

There's also Ashton Bailey, my first love. I know you've been thinking about him. I know he's been playing on your mind. I grant you, it does seem rather strange, after thirteen years of absence, that he suddenly shows up on my doorstep. Today of all days. I don't know where he lives, he made sure of that, but it must be close enough for him to get here in a hurry. Or was he already in the vicinity, and if so, why?

Could my first love be my killer?

It'd sure provide a nice, neat ending, leaving my family intact and laying blame at the man who treated me so shabbily so long ago. Except, here's the thing. He didn't really treat me shabbily, not in retrospect. Ashton was just young. He wanted to move on. He wanted to go out with other girls. Where's the crime in that?

Yet I couldn't handle it. Not one bit. He's not exaggerating about that. For three agonising years, I wouldn't let him go. I *did* stalk the guy on and off, sending mushy letters and leaving pleading phone messages, begging him to take me back.

Nothing evil, I can assure you, nothing malicious or nasty. I was trying to win him back, not freak him out although it's obvious that I did. Poor Ash. For three whole years, I just couldn't face the truth, that he no longer loved me, that he no longer wanted me in his life.

Then I did!

I promise, dear reader, I came to my senses and I walked away—and into an Irish bar where I met Cassowary Jones and fell pregnant with Bob.

The last time Ashton heard from me was thirteen years ago, closer to fourteen now that I think about it. So why show up today of all days and take his revenge? Bob's not his kid, in case that's what you're thinking (wouldn't that have thrown a spanner in the works?). Ashton never let me touch him again after that clumsy break-up sex in my dorm room that dreadful night, one eye dripping black mascara, my nose running with snot.

I get that Ash was angry, and I understand why he wanted me dead, but I really can't see him doing it. He was struggling to face me postmortem. I can't imagine he had the guts to stab me while I was alive even if it was in the back.

Besides, I'm looking at him now, down on my street, walking away again, and he's got white Volleys on his feet.

So much for that.

Don't lose heart. We're not out of suspects yet. What about Mrs Oliver? Is she a wolf in sheep's clothing? What about the middle-aged couple, are they smiling assassins? Or the tattooed stoner, is he really as hopeless as he makes out?

No, no, no, it's all completely wrong. The only neighbour I can see doing it is Psycho Sarah, and her motive is not convincing enough, not when you really think about it.

Maybe she hated me for introducing Jennifer to her sister. *Maybe* she blamed me for enabling their "disgusting" relationship, even though I didn't do it deliberately and was as surprised as she was. *Maybe* it had more to do with Henrietta kissing Bob. Yet none of that is bad enough to push you to murder. Why bother? They all would have found each other eventually or someone else entirely. I don't have that kind of power over other people, and neither does Sarah, no matter what we think.

She's not really psychotic, Sarah, in case you hadn't twigged. She's just a big bully who likes to throw her weight around, but when it comes to the crunch—when she has a chance to slam Jennifer in public, for instance, in front of her own son no less—she's a lightweight. By shuffling those kids off to the police station, Sarah threw in the towel. Better than that, she threw her opponent a life raft.

She's not as bad as she makes out.

Besides, Sarah must know, as I now do, that you can't manipulate true love, no matter how much you bluster or how many sobbing letters you send, or how wildly you dance with the curtains open in the dead of night.

Poor Cass, he loved me too much.

Poor Ash, he never loved me enough.

And poor, poor Bob. He loved me unconditionally, but he was growing up, he was growing away, and I couldn't handle it. I was the bully. I was the psychopath. It's probably just as well I'm dead, because I was killing him softly without even realising it.

And so I am left hovering above my street with no acceptable suspects and no way to save my son, whose only crime, it seems to me, was a silly little kiss in a cosy tree house on a warm summer's night.

Which brings us full circle back to the kiss, the place where it all started and where it all went off the rails.

CHAPTER 46

A Tawny Frogmouth swoops past my bedroom window, a poinciana branch tilts towards my door. A stray piece of police tape floats in the cooling breeze as the last of the crime scene heroes evacuate.

They have packed up their cameras and evidence bags, they have removed the rest of the tape, they have agreed to meet back at headquarters, and the last man out locks my door without a second glance. They're already moving on, wondering what they'll have for dinner.

Margie Oliver is pulling on warm slippers and settling in front of *Survivor* while the stoner is now snoring on his couch, despite someone screaming about "hos and bitches" from the stereo. The middle-aged couple have vanished, as have Jennifer and Fiona. Oh, no, I stand corrected. There they are, almost out of sight, back at Sarah's granny flat, where Fiona is piling clothes into a suitcase, laughing as she does it. She's not leaving town, she's moving in with Jen until she can get a place of her own. I already know she'll end up staying there and her sister will eventually come round. Will even hold the bouquet when they get hitched, just two weeks after the Australian government finally wakes up to itself and legislates equal marriage.

Don't ask me why I know these things. I just do. Take my word for it.

What I don't know is where Ashton has gone or what

his future holds. It's still so raw I'm not sure he'll ever let me see. But Brenda is back in her kitchen, poking at a delicious-looking lasagne, while Beatrice sits on the couch patiently listening to my mother who's returned to wax lyrical about me.

"She was such a beautiful bub," I can hear Dot croak. "Such a delightful child."

I'm not sure where Gertrude has got to, but I leave them to it for now. I don't need to hear any more. I know what happens next.

And I know that Mum will be joining me soon— sooner than she thinks—which is why she looks so radiant and is shining with bright light. We all do, apparently, the weeks before we die. I'll be the one to help her across, by the way. I'm taking over the mantle from Grandma, and it will be my honour. I will do so with a comforting smile.

For now, though, I'm glad Mum's having dinner with the Joneses and they are comforting each other on this dreadful, dreadful night.

And so I step outside, I take a deep breath, I inhale the early evening air, and that's when a simple sentence floats towards me on the fragrant breeze. It's the last thing my son ever said to me. Did I listen properly?

"Mum, I'm so sorry. I never should have kissed Henny. I only did it to scare her off, but it didn't..."

But. It. Didn't.

An icy chill trickles down my spine.

Bob wasn't kissing Henrietta because he *liked* her. He was kissing Henrietta to scare *someone else* away. Oh the irony! My son had a stalker.

That's why his best friend let him kiss his girlfriend.

"She was just faking it, and you got sucked in like everyone else."

The three mates were working together to scare someone else off, a fourth party, but it didn't work. That's the ominous bit—it did not work. Whoever she was, whatever she wanted, she was still hanging around Bob.

She was still stalking him, just like I had stalked Ash.

And she clearly terrified him, just as I terrified Ash. Does she terrify him still?

My heart goes into a tailspin, and my brain goes into overdrive. I haven't got time to waste. This is not about me anymore. Perhaps it never was. This is about my son and a girl who is scaring the life out of him.

This is about Bob's safety.

I think of all the girls who have been sniffing around lately. Yana, Eloise, Fran, Mary McIntyre… I can't see any of them doing it. I just can't.

I swoop away impatiently, back down my street. I want to fly to that blasted tree house, I want to rummage for clues, but it's out of reach to me, and I am stuck at the edge of my life, just up from the shabby skate park with nothing but unanswered questions to keep me company.

I want to scream. I want to wail. I want to know who has been menacing my son!

Is this karma, Grandma? Is this what it's all about? Witnessing my own karmic punishment, my son's karmic demise?

Am I reaping what I sowed? Is Bob paying the price?

I sigh with anguish. I can't seem to move past this blasted skate park where the bored teenagers still loiter despite the encroaching dark. One is doing tricks on his board, the others watch from the edge of the quarter-pipe, another lurks under a mango tree, her Converse sneakers crossed at the ankles, sucking on a flaxen plait.

I stop. I stare. And finally I see.

CHAPTER 47

Rule 4: *Thou shall see all when thou is open to seeing*

It is a dark and stormy night. Okay, forget the stormy part, but you get the picture. It is dark. I see my son, my achingly beautiful son, as he makes his way towards a muddy patch of earth in just a meagre sliver of moonlight. He pulls out his iPhone, and I am glad of it. It has a torch inside; he will need it to light his way. He could also use it to call for help if need be.

"Hey, Bobby!" someone calls out, and he turns. He frowns. My heart is in a vise, but he does not look too worried.

"Where you goin'?" she calls again.

"Nowhere! Go home!" Then more gently. "Please, I told you before, you gotta stop following me."

But she does not go home. She continues to follow. And he does not know or does not care, for he never looks back. He is in a hurry, hands thrust into his denim jacket, shoulders hunched against the wind as he dashes past the local store, across the street and down three blocks to the village hall.

There is no film showing tonight, there is not a soul about, and he does not stop there. He runs on, down to the park behind the hall, where he makes a beeline for the tree house.

There is somebody in there already. It looks like a large

man, waiting in the dark.

I stiffen further as Bob steps inside.

I follow him in and relax. It is not a man. It is Sebastian and, tucked under his arm, Henrietta. They look up at Bob expectantly, as do I, but he only smiles and says, "Hey you two, get a room!"

They laugh, break apart and greet him with a hug. He is not angry with them. He is not hurt. He is not looking betrayed.

"Happy birthday, man!" says Sebastian.

"Sorry about your mum," adds Henny.

He shrugs. "Yeah well, you know what she's like."

And now my shoulders stiffen again, but it's okay. I'm just bracing myself for the truth. Before he can say anything else, though, three more faces appear at the door. It is Jayden, Parker and Mary whose thick red curls look like busted bedsprings in the dark.

They swap greetings and tumble in, squishing everyone up in the process.

"Did you bring it?" Bob asks Henrietta, his eyes shiny with expectation, and I think, what? Did you bring what? Cigarettes? Alcohol? Pot?

She smiles and turns to a basket wedged between her feet, opens the lid and pulls out a plate of six cupcakes. They are the prettiest things I have ever seen, clad in hot-pink paper cups with gooey vanilla icing and brightly coloured sprinkles. A fat strawberry has been wedged in the top of each one, except for the middle cake.

It has a candle in it.

"My Aunty Fi made them," she says, sounding proud. "She said to say happy birthday."

He laughs. "Cool. Tell her thanks. Thanks so much!"

She hands him his cupcake, then distributes the rest around the group while Sebastian pulls out a lighter which he uses to ignite the candle in the middle of Bob's cake.

Then, on some silent directive, they break into a raucous rendition of the "Happy Birthday" song. I watch, heartbroken, as my son's friends sing the song they should have sung at his party earlier today.

They are singing with wide smiles, and Bob is beaming back. There is none of the awkwardness you usually associate with kids singing together around a cake. They are now yelling the words out, they are owning this song, they are offering it as a gift to my son, and he couldn't be happier. He looks as though he has never heard anything so brilliant.

And I guess I never have either.

It ends with a rousing applause and a slapping of Bob's back, and I watch as they all wait for Bob to remove the candle and take his first bite. Only when he has done so, only when he has chewed and given the thumbs-up do they bite from their own cupcakes, their lips plastered with icing, crumbs dropping to their laps.

They're all laughing now, shoving the cake in, except for Bob. He has tears welling in his eyes, and I know why.

He is thinking, "You could have been here, Mum, this could have been you."

And I know he is right, and I know it didn't have to be this way. He shouldn't have had to eat cake sneakily in a hutch at midnight.

I know what comes next. I know they stay an hour, joking and talking and bitching about me. I know Bob does it through gritted teeth. I know he takes no pleasure in it, but he needs it nonetheless. It's his respite from me. And I'm glad of it. I am glad of these good friends who gave him the space.

So I leave them to it. I feel like an intruder now. And I hover outside, wanting to accompany Bob home when his party is complete. That's when I see her, standing in the shadows, just behind a jagged clump of lantana. She's hovering too; she's listening in.

I hear the words, "I can't believe she wouldn't let you have your own birthday cake."

And, "What a bish!" and "I should shove that cake in

her face."

I'm not worried about them anymore, but I know she is.

She hears the words too. She formulates a plan.

And so Bob's fate is sealed, and my life is almost over.

CHAPTER 48

"**D**o you want to tell me what really happened now?" This is Detective Chasin, and he is seated across from Bob. It is late afternoon, and Bob has been crying. "You can't help her now, son, you just have to tell the truth."

"You have to tell the truth," echoes Cass, who is seated beside his son. "You need to do it for Mum, yeah?"

Bob nods, a fat tear trickling between the freckles on his cheeks.

"I should've locked the window," he says, his voice almost a whisper. He looks at his dad. "That's how she got in."

Cass nods and Chasin says, "She's come in before?"

"Just once. Or once that I knew of. Found her sleeping on the floor by my bed a few weeks ago. Totally freaked me out."

"And you found her this morning?"

He nods again. "Didn't even know she was there until Mum knocked on my door. She always wakes me on Sunday mornings. We have breaky together. It was our thing."

He doesn't sound bitter about that or angry or sad. If anything he sounds proud. It makes my heart swell.

"She was asleep on the floor, and I freaked. I told her she had to get out before Mum saw her. That Mum would kill us both if she got caught, but she kept saying, 'It's okay, Bobby. I just wanted you to have it.' And that's when I saw it."

"The cake?"

He nods. "It was on my desk."

"With the knife?" This is Tandia, and he nods again.

He sniffs. "She must have snuck in really late last night after I got back, then taken it from the fridge. She kept saying, 'It's your cake, Bobby. You should have your cake. I wanted to make sure you had it.'"

"Then what did you do?" asks Chasin.

"I didn't want the cake. It was never about the bloody cake! I told her to piss off. I told her she was a freak." He sniffs louder. "I shouldn't't've said that, I know that, I must have made her angry! But she wouldn't go, she just picked up the knife and started cutting the cake into lots of little pieces and saying, 'Your mum's a bitch like mine, but I can help you. No one ever helped *me*, but I'll look after *you*. Let's celebrate together now, Bobby. We don't need them. We don't need anyone.' I told her to shut up, that mum wasn't a bitch and she should just piss off and leave me alone."

He sobs for a moment, and Cass leans across and gently pats his back while Chasin patiently waits for my son to gather himself.

After a few minutes, Chasin prompts him again. "Then what happened?"

Bob wipes his nose with his sleeve. "Then I told her I was going downstairs and she had five minutes to get the hell out. I told her I'd distract Mum so she couldn't hear her sneaking down the stairs, and that's what I did. I went down and I flicked on the telly so Mum wouldn't hear the front door open and shut."

"So *you* turned that TV on?" asks Tandia.

"Mmm. But as soon as I went into the kitchen, I realised that Mum could probably still see her sneak out. I knew I had to shut that internal door. So when Mum started saying all this stuff about me moving out, I knew she was full of shit, but I pretended to be really angry so I could storm out, you know?"

"You *weren't* angry with your mother?" says Cass.

Bob shakes his head. "Nah, you know what she's like, Dad. She wouldn't've kicked me out."

Cass nods. No, of course not.

"So then?" Chasin says, trying to keep it on track.

"So then I stormed out and slammed the door. I just wanted to shut that kitchen off. And I wanted to get back up to my room, make sure the freak was gone. And I thought she was!" He gulps, looks ready to burst into tears again, but Cass pats his back again and he steadies himself. Breathes in. "I thought she must've snuck back out the window or something. I didn't realise… I didn't know!"

Then he does dissolve into tears, and again the detective waits it out.

"Did you notice that the cake knife was no longer in your bedroom?" he eventually asks. "Did you see the knife at that point?"

Bob looks up from the desk, confused. "I don't remember. I don't know. I didn't think…"

Chasin lets it drop. "Do you have any idea where she might have been hiding?"

"No! But she must have followed me straight down when I went to breakfast, must have been hiding just outside the kitchen because I reckon she heard what Mum said. I reckon she heard Mum tell me I had to move in with Dad, and I think that was like the final straw or something…" He breaks off again, sobbing into his elbow while Cass leans across and tries to hide him in a hug.

Detective Chasin coughs, clearing his throat. "You're doing a really good job, Bob. Please, hang in there, we're nearly done. I need you to tell me what happened next."

Bob remains huddled in the protective arms of his father.

Chasin says, "For your mum, mate."

That makes him look up through watery eyes. He nods, swipes at those eyes with his sleeve, and says, "I thought she must have left. I didn't know she was still there. I didn't go back down until that policeman rang the doorbell, the one who helped me find Mum."

"So you never went back downstairs until then?"

"No! I wish I had! If I had, maybe… Oh shit, man. She was always such a weirdo! She was such a freak, but I didn't know she was, like, *dangerous* or anything. I didn't know she would do *that*!"

"*Why* do you think she did it, Bob?" Tandia asks softly, and he looks at her as though she just asked the meaning of life.

"I… don't… know. I've been trying to work that out. That's why I didn't think it could be her. I mean, I know she had a thing for me, but I didn't think she'd do *that*…"

"But didn't you say she'd been stalking you, Bob?" says Chasin. "She'd snuck into your room uninvited, right? How long do you think this had all been going on?"

He shrugs. "I don't know, but it got worse after Mum invited her over. She thought she was my girlfriend suddenly or something. It was creepy, you know? She's so much older than me, why would she think that? That's why Henny agreed to kiss me at film night when everyone was around. We were trying to pretend I already had a girlfriend so she'd just back off. But it just made everything worse. The next day she stormed up to Henny and she ripped the thing out of her hair and called her a witch. If it wasn't for Sebastian, well, I don't know what she would have done…"

"The yellow headband?" Tandia clarifies. "You're talking about the one we found near the TV in the living room? This one?" She pushes one of the evidence bags across the table. He doesn't bother to look at it as he nods.

"Do you think she might have placed it in the living room on her way out? Maybe to frame Henrietta Burleigh?" Tandia asks, and he looks horrified at this.

"Maybe, yeah." He shrinks back. "Oh, shit, what if she had… What if…?"

He doesn't finish those sentences, but I know what he's thinking. What if Henrietta had been blamed for my murder? Or worse, what if she had been stabbed instead of me?

Thank God for small mercies.

Cass must be thinking the same thing. He is saying, "It's okay, son, it's not your fault. None of this is your fault."

"How can you say that, Dad?" Bob pushes him away, his eyes wild, his hair tufted up. "I should've known she was psycho! She kept following me everywhere! Jesus, she snuck into my room twice!"

"Why didn't you tell me, son? Why didn't you tell your mum?"

He's shaking his head. "I tried to. But I thought she'd go crazy. You know what Mum's like. I just thought, okay, I'll keep the window locked and then she can't get in, but I must have forgotten to lock it last night." He sniffs. "I should have just walked her out when I found her this morning. I should have made sure she pissed off and that Mum was safe. I should have gone back into the kitchen! I should have had breakfast with Mum! It's what we do. Every Sunday! It's our *thing*!"

And once again he falls apart sobbing.

"It's okay, Bob," Cass says, reaching a hand back to his son, but again Bob pushes him away.

"No! It's not okay! It's all my fault, don't you see? I didn't *want* to have breakfast with Mum. I wanted to punish her for not letting me have a party and not letting me have my stupid fuckin' cake! Why did I do that? If only I had gone straight back to the kitchen! I might have been able to stop her. I might have been able to save Mum."

"Oh Bobby boy, it's not your fault," Cass is saying, his voice cracking with despair, and I am nodding like a madwoman from up above.

No Bob, it's not your fault. Not one bit. And it's not even that silly girl's fault either, not really. She just thought she was protecting you in her stupid, muddled up, misguided way. She must have loved you as maniacally as I did, as dangerously too.

Detective Chasin is standing up. "I think that's enough for now. Thank you Bob, I know that was hard." He looks at Tandia. "Let's get that statement printed up and signed, then Bob can get home where he belongs, okay?"

Bob just drops his head back into his elbow and sobs his little heart out again.

CHAPTER 49

I know my time here is almost done. I know the clock is ticking down, but I need to watch this final bit. I need to know my son is safe. And so I turn back to the light.

"Just a few more minutes, please," I beg. "Just five more minutes to say good-bye."

Now it's Grandma's turn to put her thumb up. And so I am allowed to watch as one squad car weaves its way towards my house while another pulls up in front of the skate park. I can see two people sitting in the back. I have never seen either of them in anything less than a Mercedes before. They look incongruous in that dumpy police vehicle, and yet I am not surprised. And I am not surprised by the panic that's now etched into their faces. I guess they're not thinking about work anymore.

I watch as officers Paul and Megan step out of the car and towards the children who have stopped watching the skateboarder and now hold their boards like shields to their chests. But they're not staring at the police officers, they're staring towards the back of the park, to the distant mango tree, to the girl who has been lurking from the beginning, just out of reach, watching everything from a distance, a sad smile on her lips.

Fran stands as the officers approach and dusts herself off, clearly resigned to her fate. She patiently listens to what Megan says, then lets Paul lead her towards the police vehicle, towards her parents, whose sudden desperate concern is too little, too late.

How ironic, I think. One child destroyed with too much love, one with not enough.

Fran will need so much more than love now. I don't know if she was born troubled or if her up upbringing made her that way, but she will need serious psychiatric help and I hope, despite everything, that she will be okay. After all, is she really the enemy? Can we really blame her for this when all she thought she was doing was protecting my son?

I don't know how it started or how long it went on, but at some stage, for some reason, Fran assumed the role of my son's guardian angel, perhaps because she never had one of her own. It's why she mentioned the cigarette, snuck the cake to his bedroom, and stabbed his mum in the back. She was trying to save Bob from himself and then from me.

Perhaps Fran saw the way I clung to him, the way I curbed his freedom and pushed his mates away. I don't know exactly what the trigger was, but I know that somehow, at some stage, she began to believe she was Bob's protector and she needed to protect him from the enemy. Me. Yet the fact remains, Fran also needed protecting, and the people who should have done that let her down badly.

They let us all down, and now our children will pay.

But I won't waste any more time on them; they have taken enough from me, they have taken enough from Bob. Instead, I want to go back to my son, who is just getting out of a second police car, his father wedged like his conjoined twin beside him, unable to let go.

I watch as Gertrude appears first, from behind the house where she's been sobbing quietly in a hammock, missing her good mate who told her all about his creepy stalker then swore her to secrecy. I know Gertie wishes she had spoken up now and wonders if she could have saved me from my fate, but she'll get over that.

Kids are so resilient, aren't they?

Seconds later, Brenda bursts from the front door, followed quickly by Beatrice, and they all run towards Bob and Cass, pulling them into a hug so tight I think all five will suffocate. No one is speaking now, they are just hugging and crying, but I know what they are thinking and I know they are right.

Bob will be okay, he will somehow put this behind him, and he will move on with his life because he has people who love him just enough.

He has people who love him, in just the right way.

And so it is I turn away from my old life and towards the light.

I am ready, I tell Grandma, take me, I'm all yours. But again she holds a hand up. Again she says, "Not so fast."

Then she smiles her cheeky smile and says, "It's not quite over yet, my dear, you've forgotten the best part."

CHAPTER 50

Rule 7: Thou shall be granted one final wish upon entering the light

Goodness me, how could I forget that!

"My sentiments, exactly," says Grandma. "It's the greatest gift of all, you silly dill. You get a wish, one wish, to follow you into eternity."

I smile. "Ah yes. Perfect."

I think of all the things I would have wished for once.

To be alive again.

To watch Bob forever.

To return as a bird that can nest by his window.

To always know he will be okay.

I would have wished for Bob to never forget me, to think of me from the moment he awoke to the moment he went to sleep. I would have kept suffocating him, even after death.

Not anymore.

I think of all the things I would have thought of this time yesterday, all the things that consumed me back then. I would have wished only bad things for Ashton and Cass and Brenda and Todd and all the other people who didn't love me the way I needed to be loved. I would have damned them to hell and back.

Not anymore.

I don't wish for any of those things now, and I marvel

that I ever would. There is only one thing I want. There is only one thing that really matters.

I smile at Grandma and I say, "I wish for Bob to have a long, happy life."

She raises her eyebrows. "You sure about that? You know what that will mean, don't you? You won't see Bob again for another eighty years, maybe more. It'll be very lonely up here. You'll miss him dreadfully, just like I miss your mum. Is that what you really want?"

"Not at all," I reply, smiling sadly. "It's the last thing I want. But for once in my life I'm not doing what I want. I'm doing what is right."

For once in my life I am thinking of someone else. It is the purest thought I have ever had, and it will keep me company until it is Bob's turn to shuffle off this mortal coil and join me in the ever after.

I just hope that when he gets here he can forgive me for everything. For crowding him so badly, for overreacting to things I should have rejoiced in, for not trusting or listening or allowing him to breathe. I hope he can see that I loved him so much, too much. I hope he can forgive me for that.

Fran might have killed me, but it was my obsession that made it happen.

"You've done a lot of growing up, my darling," Grandma whispers, and I sigh.

"Pity it took me so long. Pity I had to drop dead to do it."

Then I take my grandmother's beautiful, withered hand, I turn away from my beloved boy, and I step into the light.

EPILOGUE

Hey, you still there? Thank goodness! I just wanted a final word. I wanted to thank you for your time, for helping me solve my murder and move across.

I know that these few hours we've spent together weren't just about saving Bob Gold. I saved myself in the process, didn't I? Perhaps I was selfish, then, right until the bitter end. Perhaps that's why Grandma chipped in to help. She couldn't stomach the idea of spending forever with the old Ludovica, and I can't say I blame her.

What a horror I was! When did I become so mean and judgmental and *smug*? I was my own worst nightmare, a tweenie girl in woman's clothing, a bulldozer in a china shop, completely oblivious to the wreckage I left behind, to the impact I had on others.

Oh well, you live and learn, right? Or, in my case, you live and die.

Anyway, enough of that, I didn't mean to get maudlin again. I just wanted to let you know I'm okay. Really I am.

It's pretty wonderful up here, you know. Like nothing I had ever expected. I won't tell you more. I wouldn't want to ruin the surprise, but suffice it to say, it's every dream you never had and nothing you ever imagined.

I've been hanging out with that loony lady and her Elvis friend. We have more in common than you'd think. They bring out my cheeky side again. They call me Mad King Ludwig and have helped me build the craziest castle you've ever seen. We have soaring steeples and crystal chandeliers, not a gaudy orange light in sight but plenty of white wicker furniture that never, ever needs painting. Brenda will love it (although she's not due for a long time, and I'm glad of that).

Grandma drops by to see how I'm doing from time to time, brings me some of her mate's liquorice, and we reminisce about mum and dad, and Bob and Cass, and all the silly little things I was once consumed by.

I know now that they are but a step on an incredible journey, and that love is an evolving process that doesn't start and stop with one guy, not even a guy called Bob. I'm looking forward to seeing him again though, but I'm in no rush. And I'll be a lot more enlightened next time, a lot more chilled out. Might even bake him a chocolate cake to welcome him across. It will be our little joke. I think he'll get it.

How about you? Did you learn from my mistakes? I hope you've been looking at your partner a little more closely lately, noticing the feathers, watching out for the dance. And I hope you've been giving your kids a little more space if they need it and a little more attention if they don't.

I hope you chat more to your neighbours and leave old flames and married bosses alone, and I hope you remember that while you may sometimes feel lonely, you are never truly alone.

So thanks again, so long, and may your passage through the tunnel be a little less eventful than mine. I mean, seriously, haven't you had enough excitement for one lifetime?

~~~
~~~

ALSO BY C.A. LARMER

After the Ferry: A Psychological Novel

IT'S THE 1990s, pre-mobile phones, and a young traveller must make a terrifying choice: Will she jump ship with a seductive stranger? Or stay cocooned on the Greek ferry with friends and miss what could be the love of her life?
One choice leads to true love.
One choice leads to murder.
But which is which?

"Larmer's plot is a clever one…The characters are finely honed and credible, and Amelia's contrasting lives and personalities are brilliantly rendered and made plausible."
Jack Magnus, Readers Favorite

Killer Twist (Ghostwriter Mystery 1)

KILLER TWIST is the first stand-alone mystery in the popular 'amateur women sleuths' series featuring feisty ghostwriter Roxy Parker.

"A fun read with a well defined protagonist, interesting secondary characters and an easy style. Lots of local flavour which catches the imagination."
Parents' Little Black Book @ Amazon

"Roxy Parker is a compelling character and I couldn't help but adore her. She's 30, hip, very inquisitive, and fiercely independent. A great cozy. I enjoyed it immensely and will be ordering the second in the series."
Rhonda @Amazon

calarmer.com

9 780099 426086